Emric Ladislas

I Tried

I dived into the depths of danger, plunging into the unknown just for you, yet…

I Tried

Text copyright © Joseph Jethro

All rights reserved. No part of this publication may be reproduced, distributed, or transmitted in any form or by any means, including photocopying, recording, or other electronic or mechanical methods, without the author's prior written permission. Such written permission must also be obtained before any part of this publication is stored in a retrieval system.

All characters of this publication are fictitious, and any resemblance to actual persons, living or dead, is purely coincidental.

First published in Great Britain in 2024

ISBN: 978-1-917452-16-8

josephjethro45@outlook.com

Contents

Chapter 1 6
Check ma whip out! 6
Chapter 2 12
Wanna take ma babe for a spin?........................12
Chapter 3 16
Cut the envy, man! It ain't good for ya!.............16
Chapter 4 21
Ya need yer fix? I need ma cash! 21
Chapter 5 26
Get lost, Jareth! 26
Chapter 6 31
Remember me, please! 31
Chapter 7 41
Check out yer jalopy! 41
Chapter 8 47
Damn it! You gotta dig deeper! 47
Chapter 9 52
I can make it right! I swear! 52
Chapter 10 63
My life's just messed up! 63

Chapter 11 68
I've lost you forever! 68
Chapter 12 83
I promise to make you proud! 83

More Titles By Joseph Jethro:

- Undercover Gangster: Blood Ties In The Shadows
- Secret Gangster: My Life Is All About Violence
- Triple Caste Gangster: He Never Told Her
- Never Underestimate Girls: Will She Ever Unlock The Truth or…

Chapter 1
Check ma whip out!

Brander sat comfortably in his cosy living room, the soft glow of the evening sun filtering through the curtains. His legs were casually propped up on the coffee table, a position he found most relaxing after a long day. The room was filled with the faint aroma of freshly brewed tea, mingling with the subtle scent of the lavender candle flickering on the mantelpiece.

With a contented sigh, Brander picked up his phone, his fingers deftly swiping through various apps and notifications. His other hand absentmindedly traced the delicate rim of his teacup, the warmth of the ceramic, a comforting contrast to the cool air which blew through the open window. A smile played on his lips as he thought of his friend, Emric.

'Emric,' he chuckled softly, a smile playing on his lips. He browsed the Audi dealership's website, his excitement almost tangible. 'I can't wait to show you my new car!' he murmured, envisioning the astonishment and admiration that would light up Emric's face. The anticipation of sharing his joy with his friend added a vibrant layer of happiness to his evening, making his heart race eagerly.

Brander's excitement grew as he continued to browse the Audi dealership's website. He leaned forward, his eyes scanning the sleek images of various models. Each car seemed more impressive than the last, but he was looking for something special, something that would truly stand out.

After a few moments of scrolling, he was captivated by the picture of the Audi Q8. The car's bold, aggressive lines and luxurious design immediately caught his interest. He clicked on the image, bringing up a detailed view of the vehicle. The Q8's wide stance and imposing framework displayed confidence and power, while the elegant curves and sophisticated finish held his attention.

Brander's fingers danced over the screen as he explored the car's features. The interior was a masterpiece of modern design, with plush leather seats and bright lighting. He could almost feel the smooth leather under his fingertips and hear the crisp sound of the premium audio system. The panoramic sunroof, which stretched across the entire length of the cabin, promised breathtaking views and a sense of openness.

Brander couldn't wait any longer. He quickly navigated to the dealership's contact page and dialled the number. As he waited for someone to answer, his eyes wandered around the living room, his mind already racing ahead to the moment he would drive his new car home.

'Good evening, Audi dealership; how can I assist you?' a friendly voice answered.

'Hi, I'd like to inquire about the Audi Q8,' Brander said, his voice brimming with excitement. 'I'm very interested in purchasing one.'

The conversation flowed smoothly, with the salesperson providing all the information Brander needed. They discussed the various customisation options, from the exterior colour to the interior finishes. Brander opted for a deep metallic blue, which he felt perfectly matched his personality. He chose the premium leather seats in an elegant, rich brown shade and incorporated a few extra options, like the advanced sound system and the sports package.

Brander felt a sense of satisfaction and excitement. He would soon be the proud owner of a stunning Audi Q8.

As Brander hung up the phone, he heard the soft, rhythmic tap of someone's footsteps against the cool, polished marble floor in

I Tried

the hallway. He looked up to see his wife, Elara, entering the room with a curious smile.

'Hey, love,' she greeted, settling into the armchair opposite him. 'You look like you've got some exciting news. What's up?'

Brander's face lit up with enthusiasm. 'I just finalised the details for our new car. It's an Audi Q8, and it's absolutely stunning.'

Elara raised an eyebrow, intrigued. 'An Audi Q8? That sounds impressive. Tell me more about it.'

Brander leaned forward, his excitement evident. 'It's got this incredible design, bold and elegant at the same time. The interior is luxurious, with plush leather seats and a panoramic sunroof. I decided on a deep metallic blue finish for the exterior and elegant brown for the seats. And the features! Advanced driver assistance systems, a premium sound system, and even a sports package.'

Elara smiled, clearly impressed. 'It sounds amazing. I can't wait to see it.'

Brander continued, 'And you know what? I can't wait to show it to Emric. He's always been such a car enthusiast. I can already picture his face when he sees it. He'll be thrilled.'

Elara chuckled. 'Emric will probably want to take it for a spin the moment he lays his eyes on it.'

'Absolutely,' Brander agreed, laughing. 'He's been talking about getting a new car himself, but I think this will blow him away. I can't wait to take him for a ride and see his reaction.'

Elara reached over and squeezed Brander's hand. 'I'm so happy for you, Brander. You deserve this. And I'm sure Emric will be just as excited as you are.'

Brander's hands tightened on his brand-new car's sleek, leather-wrapped steering wheel as he sped down the winding roads. The engine roared with power, sending a thrill through his

I Tried

veins. The sun was setting, casting a golden hue over the landscape, and the car's polished exterior gleamed in the fading light.

He sensed the ride's smooth flow, the meticulous control of the handling, and the sheer force of acceleration as he pressed down on the gas pedal. The car responded instantly, surging forward with a burst of speed that made his heart race. He was on his way to pick up his best mate, eager to show off his latest acquisition.

As he navigated the bends, Brander couldn't help but smile. The car was everything he had dreamed of and more, and it was all his.

He finally got to his mate's street, where Emric was meant to be waiting. Brander pulled up in front of the house, the engine purring as he came to a stop. He saw Emric stumbling towards him with a wide grin on his face, his eyes slightly red, and his movements a bit erratic. 'Yo, like yer whip, dude!' Emric laughed, jumping into the passenger seat. 'It's spectacular, man!'

Brander chuckled, 'Told ya,' he smiled, 'I only deal in the best.'

As Brander began their journey together, Emric looked at him, 'Can ya put the window down, pal?'

'Why?' Brander asked, side-eyeing him.

Emric's hand slipped into his jeans pocket, fumbling momentarily before pulling out a crumpled pack of cigarettes and a small baggie of something else. 'Ya see,' he said, pulling out a cig and lighting it with a shaky hand, 'I need to have this. And maybe a lil' somethin' extra.'

Brander rolled his eyes, 'Druggy,' he muttered, lowering the window.

He watched as Emric sparked up and started to enjoy himself, taking heavy drags and exhaling clouds of smoke. The smell of tobacco filled the car, mingling with the new car scent. Emric

I Tried

leaned back, a look of bliss on his face as he took another drag. 'This is the life, man,' he said, his voice slightly slurred. 'You and me, cruisin' in this beast. Nothin' better.'

Emric then pulled out something else and started to roll it, his hands shaking slightly. 'Gotta have my fix, ya know?' he mumbled, more to himself than to Brander. He lit up the new roll and inhaled deeply. 'Ah, that's the stuff,' he sighed, sinking deeper into the seat.

Brander couldn't help but smile despite the smoke and his friend's slightly concerning behaviour. He pressed down on the gas pedal, the car roaring as they sped down the road, the wind whipping through the open window.

The city lights blurred past them, creating a kaleidoscope of colours in the night. Emric, now more relaxed and slightly dazed, leaned back in his seat, his head lolling to the side as he took another deep drag from his makeshift joint.

'Man, this ride is somethin' else,' Emric slurred, his eyes half-closed. 'Feels like we're flyin'.'

Brander smirked, enjoying the thrill of the speed and the admiration from his friend. 'Told ya, mate. Only the best for us.'

They cruised through the city, the streets gradually becoming less crowded as they ventured further from the bustling centre. Brander took a sharp turn, the tyres squealing slightly, and Emric let out a whoop of excitement.

'Yeah, that's what I like!' Emric shouted, his voice filled with exhilaration. He fumbled with the car's sound system, managing to crank up the volume. The bass thumped through the speakers, adding to the adrenaline-fueled atmosphere.

Emric pulled out his phone, his fingers clumsily tapping on the screen. 'Gotta let the boys know 'bout this,' he mumbled, bombarding their group chat with a flurry of nonsensical messages. 'They ain't gonna believe this.'

I Tried

Brander glanced over, shaking his head with a chuckle. 'You're a mess, Emric.'

Emric laughed, a raspy sound that turned into a cough. 'Yeah,' he said, grinning widely. He took another drag, the smoke curling around his face. 'Hey, pull over here,' he suddenly said, pointing to a dimly lit alleyway.

Brander frowned but obeyed, slowing the car and turning into the narrow alley. 'What for?'

Emric rummaged through his pockets, pulling out a small vial. 'Just need a quick hit,' he muttered, his hands shaking slightly as he prepared the substance. 'Won't take long.'

Brander sighed, watching as Emric leapt out of the car and started to take his drugs. Emric's mind blanked out momentarily before he shook his head and blinked rapidly. He jumped back into the car, 'All right, let's go,' he said, his voice steadier.

They pulled back onto the main road, the car's engine roaring as Brander accelerated. The night air rushed through the open window, carrying away the lingering smoke. Emric leaned back, a contented smile on his face. 'This is the life, man,' he repeated, his voice softer. 'Just you, me, and the open road.'

Brander glanced over at his friend, concern etched on his face. 'Emric bro, you need to stop takin' drugs, man,' he said, his tone serious. 'it ain't good for ya.'

Emric looked at him, a lazy smile on his face. 'Ah, come on, man, Brander. It's just a bit of fun. Nothin' serious.'

Brander shook his head, pressing down on the gas pedal. 'It might seem like fun now, but it's gonna catch up with ya. I don't want to see you go down that path.'

Emric sighed, leaning back in his seat. 'Yeah, yeah, I hear ya,' he mumbled. 'But right now, let's just enjoy the ride, alright?'

Brander nodded, despite the persistent worry in his head. He cared about Emric and didn't want to see him get hurt.

Chapter 2
Wanna take ma babe for a spin?

Brander lay sprawled on his bed, his hazel eyes staring blankly at the ceiling. The room was dimly lit, the soft glow of his bedside lamp casting shadows on the walls. He could hear the faint hum of the city outside his window, a perpetual reminder of the bustling world around him. His mind wandered aimlessly, thoughts drifting in and out like the ebb and flow of the tide.

Suddenly, the silence was broken by the sharp ring of his phone. Startled, Brander glanced over at the screen, seeing Emric's name flashing. Sighing, he reached over and picked up the phone, running his fingers through his tousled brown hair.

'Hi,' he answered, his voice tinged with weariness. 'What's up?'

'Bruv!' Emric's voice came through the speaker, slurred but brimming with excitement. 'Got somethin' to show ya. Can ya cruise down to ma end?'

Brander could almost picture Emric on the other end, probably grinning widely. Despite his friend's usual antics, there was something about his enthusiasm. Brander couldn't help but smile a little.

'O'right,' Brander replied, rising from the bed. 'I'm on my way.'

He hung up the phone and swung his legs over the side of the bed, feeling the cool floor beneath his feet. He grabbed his jacket from the chair and donned it, the familiar weight providing comfort.

As he headed out the bedroom door, he couldn't shake the feeling of curiosity mixed with a hint of concern. Whatever

I Tried

Emric had to show him, it was bound to be interesting, if not a little chaotic.

The night air was crisp as Brander stepped outside, the city lights twinkling in the distance. He made his way to his car, the sleek machine gleaming under the streetlights. Sliding into the driver's seat, he started the engine, the powerful roar filling the quiet street. Taking a deep breath, he began his journey to Emric's place, the anticipation building with each passing mile.

Brander drove up to Emric's house, his eyes widening as he spotted a sleek, orange Lamborghini Aventador parked in front. The car's aggressive lines and low stance made it look like a predator ready to pounce. He couldn't help but admire the gleaming paintwork and the sheer presence of the vehicle.

Approaching the car, he glanced in, and his eyes widened. Emric was relaxed in the driver's seat, his golden chains glinting in the dim light. His fingers, adorned with chunky rings, clutched the steering wheel with a sense of ownership and pride. The car's interior was a mix of luxury and high-tech.

Emric rolled down the window as he noticed Brander in his Audi Q8. A cloud of cigarette smoke billowed out of the Lamborghini and filled the air with its pungent scent. 'Hey, dude!' he shouted, his voice slightly slurred. 'Like ma whip? Burn, man! Mine looks better than yours!' He laughed and then started to cough hysterically.

Brander couldn't help but chuckle. 'You always gotta get something better than me, huh?' he said, shaking his head with a smile.

Emric grinned. 'You know it, bruv. This babe's a beast. Wanna take her for a spin?'

Brander nodded, feeling a mix of excitement and concern. 'Sure, but you gotta promise me something.'

Emric raised an eyebrow, his grin faltering slightly. 'What's that?'

'No more of this,' Brander said, gesturing to the cigarette. 'You gotta cut back, man. It's not good for ya.'

Emric sighed deeply, leaning back in the plush leather seat of the Lamborghini. The gentle hum of the engine provided a soothing background noise. 'Got it, Brander,' he muttered, his voice tinged with a resigned tone. He took one last, deep drag from his cigarette, savouring the moment before flicking the smouldering butt out the window. The glowing ember flew through the air before landing on the pavement, where it fizzled out.

Brander parked his car on the curb, the engine's roar dying down to a gentle purr before he turned it off. He jumped out, the cool night air hitting him as he closed the car door. The street was quiet; all he could hear was the far-off hum of traffic and the sporadic chirping of crickets.

As Brander approached, he couldn't help but feel a surge of envy. His own car, though impressive, seemed to pale in comparison to the sheer magnificence of Emric's ride. The Lamborghini's wide, low-slung frame gave it a sense of perpetual motion, even when idle. The rims gleamed under the streetlights, and the faint smell of leather and high-end materials wafted from the open window.

Emric embodied the essence of a king in his sophisticated sports car. His golden chains glinted in the dim light, and his ringed fingers drummed a lazy rhythm on the steering wheel. He glanced up at Brander, a sluggish grin spreading across his face. 'Jealous, mate?' he teased.

Brander forced a smile, trying to push down the feeling of inadequacy as he jumped into the sports car. 'Just a bit,' he

I Tried

admitted, eyes roaming over the car's luxurious interior. 'You really outdid yourself this time.'

Emric laughed, a croaky sound. 'You know me, always gotta have the best,' he said, his eyes twinkling with mischief. 'But hey, it's not just about the car. It's about the ride, the freedom. You and me, bruv, hurtling up the streets.'

Brander couldn't help but smile at his friend's passion. 'Yeah, Emric,' he said, glancing at his mate. Emric's eyes looked dazed, and a faint smell of smoke lingered in the air. 'Just make sure you don't crash the car. You look so dazed from all the drugs you take that I can't trust ya.'

Emric flicked his hand in a dismissive gesture, his grin widening. 'Relax, man. I got this. Ain't nothin' gonna happen to this beauty.' He revved the engine, the mighty roar filling the night air. 'Besides, what's life without a little risk, eh?'

Brander shook his head, amusement and concern playing on his features. 'Just be careful, alright? This car's a beast, and I don't want to see you get hurt.'

Emric nodded, his expression softening for a moment. 'I hear ya, bruv. I'll be careful. Promise. You worry to much.' He took a deep breath, his fingers tightening on the steering wheel. 'Now, let's hit the road and show this city what we're made of.'

With that, Emric shifted the car into gear, and they sped off into the night. The Lamborghini's engine roared as they sped down the streets, the city lights blurring into a kaleidoscope of colours around them. Brander could feel the car's power beneath him, the ride's smoothness, and the thrill of speed. Despite his worries, he couldn't deny the exhilaration of the moment.

Chapter 3
Cut the envy, man! It ain't good for ya!

The world flew past in a blur, the landscape transforming into streaks of green and gold as Brander sped down the open road. The midday sun hung high in the sky, casting a warm glow over everything it touched. The mighty roar of his car's engine was a masterpiece of mechanical precision that sent a thrill through his veins. The wind whipped through the open windows, tousling his hair and carrying away the day's worries.

Brander loved nothing better than being alone in his car, the freedom of the open road stretching out before him. The smooth asphalt beneath the tyres, the responsive handling, and the sheer force of acceleration made him feel alive.

Yet, despite the delight, a nagging thought lingered in the back of his mind. He couldn't shake the feeling of dissatisfaction that Emric had a better car than him. The memory of Emric's Lamborghini Aventador, with its sleek lines and aggressive stance, gnawed at him. It was a masterpiece of automotive engineering, and no matter how much he loved his own car, it just didn't compare.

As he navigated the winding roads, Brander let the rhythm of the drive take over. The engine's roar, the rush of the wind, and the blur of the landscape give a sense of freedom. He knew that no matter what, this was his moment, his escape.

But sadness and madness began to creep in as the miles flew by. The envy and frustration he felt towards Emric's car started to consume him. He leaned forward in his seat, his knuckles white as he gripped the steering wheel. The speedometer climbed higher, the needle pushing into the red zone.

I Tried

He floored the gas, the engine roaring in response. The car surged forward, the landscape outside turning into a dizzying blur. The wind whipped through the open windows, stinging his eyes and making it hard to see. His heart pounded in his chest, a mix of adrenaline and fear coursing through his veins.

Brander's vision narrowed, the road ahead becoming a tunnel of speed and motion. He barely noticed the sharp turn coming up, his mind too clouded by the rush of emotions. The tyres screeched as he tried to make the turn, but it was too late. The car skidded, the back end fishtailing wildly.

He was overwhelmed with panic as the car skidded off the road. The world spun around him, a chaotic whirl of colours and sounds. He saw the tree too late, the massive trunk looming in front of him. There was a sickening crunch as the car slammed into the tree, the impact jarring him violently.

Brander sat in the wrecked car, his mind reeling from the impact. The vehicle's front end was crumpled against the tree, the bonnet bent and twisted. A sharp pain emitted through his chest where the seatbelt had dug in, but he was grateful it had done its job. The silence around him was oppressive, broken only by the sound of his ragged breathing.

As he tried to gather his thoughts, a faint smell of gasoline reached his nose. Panic surged through him as he realised the danger he was in. He fumbled with the seatbelt, his fingers trembling as he tried to unbuckle it. The smell grew stronger, and he saw a thin wisp of smoke curling up from the bonnet.

'Come on, come on,' he muttered to himself, finally managing to release the seatbelt. He pushed the door open with a grunt, the metal creaking in protest. But as he tried to move, a sharp pain shot through his leg. He looked down and realised his leg was pinned under the dashboard, trapped by the twisted metal.

I Tried

A tiny spark ignited beneath the bonnet, rapidly expanding as it consumed the available fuel. Brander's heart raced as he watched the fire spread, the heat becoming intense. He struggled to free his leg, but the pain was too much. He was stuck!

The flames danced around the car's engine, the fire spreading rapidly. The heat was almost unbearable, and Brander felt sweat trickling down his face. He knew he had to get out, but he was trapped. His eyesight started to blur, the edges of his vision darkening as the smoke filled the car. He coughed, the acrid smell burning his lungs. His head felt heavy, and he could feel consciousness slipping away.

The final sight before darkness consumed him was the fire inching closer, the heat becoming intolerable.

Brander's eyelids fluttered open; he realised he was on a firm mattress. The sterile smell of antiseptic filled his nose, and the soft beeping of machines surrounded him. He blinked, trying to clear the fog from his mind. His body ached all over, and he could feel the tightness of bandages around his chest and leg.

He looked around the room, confusion clouding his thoughts. Nothing seemed familiar. The walls were a stark white, and the fluorescent lights above cast a harsh glow. He tried to remember how he had gotten here, but his mind was blank.

'Brander, you're awake!' a voice said softly.

He turned his head slowly, wincing at the pain, and saw a man sitting beside him. The man's face was pale, his eyes red-rimmed with worry. 'Mate, ya gave us all a scare,' the man said, his voice trembling. 'I thought I lost ya.'

Brander stared at him, his brow furrowing in confusion. 'Who…who are you?' he stammered, his voice frail and raspy, the words blending together.

I Tried

The man's face fell, a look of shock and hurt crossing his features. 'It's me, Emric. Your best mate.'

Brander shook his head slowly, the name not ringing any bells. 'I…I don't…'member,' he said, his voice breaking and slurred. 'I don't…'member anythin'.'

A woman stepped forward, her eyes filled with tears. 'Brander, it's me, your wife,' she said softly. 'Please, try to remember.'

Brander looked at her, his heart aching at the sight of her tears, but there was no recognition. 'I'm…sorry,' he whispered, his speech halting and slurred. 'I don't…know…who you…are.'

Emric and the woman exchanged a worried glance, their concern evident. 'It's okay, Brander,' Emric said, his voice steady despite the turmoil in his eyes. 'We'll help you through this. We'll get your memory back.'

Brander stared at the man, 'I…don't…know…what…you…talkin'…bout.'

Suddenly, the door to the room opened, and a nurse stepped in, her presence bringing a sense of calm to the tense atmosphere. 'Hi,' she greeted with a warm smile, walking to Brander's bedside. 'How are you feeling today?'

Brander turned his head slowly to look at her, his eyes wide with confusion. 'Who…you…are?' he stuttered, his words muddled and slow. He struggled to form clear sentences, his mind a foggy mess.

The nurse's smile remained gentle and reassuring. 'I'm Nurse Kelly,' she said softly, placing a comforting hand on his arm. 'You're in the hospital. You were in an accident, but you're safe now. We're here to help you.'

Brander's eyes darted around the room, taking in the unfamiliar surroundings. The white walls, the beeping machines, the concerned faces of the people around him, it was all too much

I Tried

to process. 'I...don't...'member...anythin',' he mumbled, his voice barely above a whisper.

Nurse Kelly nodded understandingly. 'That's okay, Brander. You've been through a lot. It's normal to feel confused and disoriented. We're going to take good care of you.'

Emric moved closer, his eyes filled with worry. 'Yo, bro! We got your back. We'll help you ride this out, no worries!' he said, his voice steady despite the turmoil in his eyes.

Brander looked at Emric and then at the woman standing beside him, her eyes brimming with tears. 'Who...she?' he asked, his words broken and unclear.

The woman stepped forward, her voice trembling. 'I'm your wife, Brander. Please, try to remember,' she pleaded, her eyes searching his for any sign of recognition.

Brander shook his head slowly, the effort of speaking and understanding leaving him exhausted. 'I...sorry...don't... know...you,' he said, his heart hurting at the sight of her tears.

Nurse Kelly gently squeezed his arm. 'It's okay, Brander. Memory loss can happen after a traumatic event. We'll work together to help you recover,' she said reassuringly.

As Brander lay back against the pillows, the weight of his situation pressing down on him, he felt a mix of fear and helplessness. He didn't know who these people were, but he could see the love and concern in their eyes.

Chapter 4
Ya need yer fix? I need ma cash!

Emric flicked the hood of his jumper as he strolled out of the hospital, the heavy rain lashing against his face. Each drop felt like a tiny needle, cold and relentless. He hunched his shoulders, trying to shield himself from the downpour, and tucked his hands deep into the pockets of his jeans. The streets were shiny with rain, the water pooling in the gutters and reflecting the dim streetlights.

He walked briskly towards his Lamborghini, the sleek orange car standing out against the dreary backdrop. The rain drummed on the car's roof, creating a rhythmic, almost soothing sound. Emric reached the car and quickly unlocked it, the door opening with a soft click. He jumped in, the leather seat cool against his back, a stark contrast to the warmth of his body.

Inside the car, the world seemed to quiet down. The rain was still pounding outside, but the interior of the Lamborghini was a cocoon of luxury and silence. Emric took a moment to catch his breath, his mind racing with thoughts of Brander. He adjusted the rearview mirror, his reflection staring back at him, eyes filled with worry and exhaustion.

He started the car, the engine roaring to life with a powerful growl. The sound was comforting, a reminder of his control and power behind the wheel. But even as he revved the engine, his mind was elsewhere. He couldn't stop thinking about Brander, lying in that hospital bed with no memory of who he was or the life he had lived.

Emric's thoughts were a whirlwind of emotions. He felt a deep sense of guilt, wondering if there was something he could have done to prevent the accident. The image of Brander's confused and frightened face haunted him, the way he had struggled to recognise his own best friend. It was a painful reminder of how delicate life could be.

As he drove through the rain-soaked streets, the windshield wipers working furiously to keep the view clear, Emric's mind kept drifting back to the hospital room. He remembered the nurse's calm voice, the sterile smell of antiseptic, and the beeping of the machines that monitored Brander's condition. It all felt surreal, like a bad dream he couldn't wake up from.

He navigated the familiar streets, the rain blurring the city lights into a hazy glow. The usually bustling roads were nearly empty, the rain driving most people indoors. Emric's grip on the steering wheel tightened, his knuckles white with tension.

He didn't know what the future held, but he was determined to be there for Brander every step of the way. The road ahead might be uncertain, but he knew he would do everything to help his mate.

Suddenly, Emric's phone buzzed, breaking the silence inside the car. He glanced at the screen, his heart sinking when he saw the caller ID: his drug supplier. The name flashed ominously, a stark reminder of the life he was trying to leave behind. With a heavy sigh, he swiped the screen to answer the call.

'Hi,' he mumbled, a note of reluctance in his tone.

'Are you coming or not?' the man on the other end snapped, his voice brimming with impatience. 'I've been waiting for you.'

Emric sighed again, the weight of the decision pressing down on him. He didn't feel like it anymore. The last words of his beloved mate, Brander, resounded in his mind, urging him to stay away from drugs. The memory of Brander's plea, the desperation in his eyes, was still fresh and raw.

'I'm coming,' he finally sighed, the words feeling like a betrayal as they left his lips. He disconnected the call, the screen going dark, and leaned back in his seat, the leather cool against his back. The engine's steady hum was the only sound in the car, a stark contrast to the turmoil in his mind.

He parked by a crumbling warehouse on the city's outskirts, which appeared deserted but wasn't. The rain had transformed the dirt lot into a quagmire, and Emric's Lamborghini looked out of place among the dilapidated surroundings. He parked the car and took a deep breath, preparing himself for what would come.

The rain intensified as he exited the car, soaking through his hoodie. He pulled the hood tighter around his face and walked towards the entrance, his footsteps squelching in the mud. The warehouse door creaked open, and a figure emerged from the shadows.

The man was tall and gaunt, his face lined with years of hard living. His eyes were bloodshot, and his clothes hung loosely on his frame. He looked every bit the part of a seasoned drug dealer, his demeanour exuding a mix of menace and desperation.

'You're late,' the man growled, his voice rough and gravelly. He took a drag from a cigarette, the tip glowing brightly in the dim light. 'I've been waiting for you.'

Emric sighed, his resolve wavering. 'Yeah, I know. Sorry,' he muttered, avoiding the man's piercing gaze.

The dealer, known on the streets as Razor, flicked the cigarette butt into the mud and stepped closer. 'You don't look too good, Emric. What's the matter? Got cold feet?' he sneered, his breath reeking of stale smoke and alcohol.

Emric shook his head, trying to push down the rising tide of guilt. 'Nah, man, it's just…things have been rough,' he said, his voice barely above a whisper. 'Brander's in hospital. He doesn't remember anything and the last thing he said to me to stay away from this shit.'

I Tried

Razor's expression softened momentarily but quickly turned back to a sneer. 'Memory loss, huh? But you know how it is, man. Business is business. You need yer fix, and I need ma cash.'

Emric felt a wave of shame wash over him as he reached into his pocket, pulling out a wad of cash. 'Yeah, I know,' he said, handing over the money. 'Just give me what I need.'

Razor took the money, counting it with practised ease. He pulled a small baggie from his coat pocket, the contents glinting in the dim light. 'Here you go, mate. The good stuff. This'll take the edge off,' he said, his voice dripping with false camaraderie.

Emric took the baggie, his hands trembling. He knew he shouldn't be doing this, but the pull was too strong. He needed an escape, even if it was temporary. 'Thanks,' he mumbled, turning to leave.

As he returned to his car, the rain continued to pour, each drop feeling like a tiny hammer against his skin. He climbed into the driver's seat, the leather cold and unwelcoming. He stared at the baggie in his hand, the weight of his choices pressing down on him.

With a heavy sigh, Emric started the car and drove away from the warehouse.

He navigated through the maze of city streets until he found a secluded alley hidden away from prying eyes. He parked the car and stepped out, the rain still pouring down. The alley was dark and narrow, the perfect place to disappear for a while. He leaned against the cold, damp wall and pulled out the baggie, his hands shaking.

He prepared the drugs with practised ease, his mind numb to the routine. As he took the first hit, a wave of euphoria washed over him, momentarily drowning out the guilt and pain. He closed his eyes, letting the sensation take over, the world around him fading into a hazy blur.

I Tried

Emric's breathing slowed, his mind drifting into a state of calmness. The alley, once a place of shadows and fear, now felt like a sanctuary where he could escape from everything, even for a little while.

But the euphoria was fleeting. As the high began to wear off, Emric felt a gnawing emptiness inside him. He took another hit and then another, each one less satisfying than the last. The rain pounded harder, the cold seeping into his bones, but he barely noticed. He was chasing a feeling that was slipping further and further away.

His sight grew hazy, the periphery fading to black as the drugs took hold. His body felt increasingly heavy, his limbs numb and unresponsive. Panic surged through him, but it was too late. He had taken too much.

Emric's knees buckled, and he slid down the wall, collapsing onto the wet pavement. The world around him spun, the rain a distant roar in his ears. His breathing became shallow, each breath a struggle. He tried to call out for help, but his voice was lost in the storm.

As consciousness slipped away, Emric's last thoughts were of Brander, lying in the hospital bed, and the promise he had made to his friend. The darkness closed in, and he passed out, the rain washing over him, the alley silent and empty once more.

Chapter 5
Get lost, Jareth!

Emric's eyes suddenly shot open as he felt someone gently touch his shoulder. He looked up to see a pair of worried blue eyes staring at him, piercing through the haze of his drug-induced daze.

'Emric, you thick shit,' a familiar voice said, laced with a mix of frustration and worry. 'Don't tell me you overdid it again!'

Emric slowly sat up, his vision hazy and his mind struggling to focus. The effects of the drugs were still heavy on him, clouding his thoughts and making everything seem distant and strange. He squinted at the figure standing over him, trying to make sense of the blurry outline. As his vision cleared, he recognised the face of one of his mates, Jareth.

'Get lost, Jareth,' he grunted, his voice rough and unclear. 'I'll break yer face in.'

Jareth sighed, shaking his head. 'You're a mess, mate. Look at you,' he said, his tone softening. He crouched beside Emric, eyes scanning the alley for any signs of danger. 'You can't keep doing this to yourself. Brander wouldn't want this for you.'

Emric's head lolled to the side, his body feeling like lead. He knew Jareth was right, but the pull of the drugs was too strong, the need for escape too overwhelming. 'I don't need a lecture,' he muttered, trying to push Jareth away but lacking the strength.

Jareth's patience wore thin. 'You're not listening!' he snapped, grabbing Emric by the collar and shaking him. 'You're killing yourself, and for what? A bit of numbness?'

Emric's eyes flared with anger, and with a sudden burst of energy, he shoved Jareth back. 'I said, get lost!' he roared,

I Tried

staggering to his feet. The alley spun around him, but he clenched his fists, ready to fight.

Jareth stumbled but quickly regained his balance. 'Fine, you wanna fight? Come on then!' he shouted, stepping forward. The two friends squared off, their emotions boiling over.

Emric swung a clumsy punch, but Jareth dodged it easily, his reflexes sharp. 'You're too slow, mate,' Jareth taunted, landing a quick jab to Emric's ribs. Emric grunted in pain but refused to back down. He swung again, this time connecting with Jareth's shoulder, causing him to stagger back.

'Is that all you've got?' said Jareth, rubbing his shoulder. He lunged forward, tackling Emric to the ground. The two rolled in the dirt, grappling and throwing wild punches. Emric's strength was fuelled by anger and desperation, but Jareth's movements were calculated and precise.

Just as Emric managed to pin Jareth down, another figure darted between them. 'Enough!' a stern voice commanded. It was Hayton, their mutual friend, whose presence was imposing and authoritative.

'Stop this madness, both of you!' Hayton's voice was firm, his eyes blazing with determination. He turned to Emric. 'Emric, look at yourself. This isn't you. The drugs are destroying you, and you're pushing away the people who care about you!'

Emric's eyes were wild with anger and confusion. 'I don't care!' he roared. He staggered to his feet, his movements unsteady and erratic. 'I hate life, and I hate you lot the most!' His voice resonated through the narrow alley, filled with rage and despair.

Hayton's expression hardened, his frustration clear. 'You're the one who's bloody taking the drugs. You dirty druggy,' he shouted back, his voice cutting through the tension like a knife. 'You're not going to get anywhere. You can't even walk!'

I Tried

    Disregarding Hayton's warnings, Emric staggered towards his Lamborghini at the alley's end. His movements were laboured and inconsistent, each step a battle against the haze clouding his thoughts. He reached the car and fumbled with the door handle, finally managing to open it. He collapsed into the driver's seat, leaning back with a heavy sigh.
    As he sat there, the adrenaline from the confrontation began to wear off, and his mind started to clear. Memories of Brander, the mindless man, flooded back to him. The once lively and energetic Brander was now in the hospital, struggling to speak like a baby learning its first words.
    'Brander,' he whispered to himself, the name a painful reminder of his actions. He remembered Brander's lectures, the countless times he had tried to warn him about the dangers of drugs. Brander's words had always been filled with genuine concern, a stark contrast to the anger and frustration of others.
    Emric's eyes welled up with tears as he thought about his friend. He never minded Brander telling him to stop, but he hated it when other people said it. Brander always spoke from a place of compassion and empathy, rather than judgment.
    Emric's trembling hands gripped the steering wheel as he eased the sleek Lamborghini onto the road. The engine purred beneath him, a harmonious blend of power and precision. The familiar leather scent of the car's interior surrounded him, mingling with the acrid residue of the drugs he had consumed earlier. Each turn of the wheel felt like a desperate attempt to regain control, to steer away from the abyss that threatened to swallow him whole.
    The streetlights flickered past, casting elongated shadows on the asphalt. Emric's mind was a whirlwind of conflicting emotions, fear, regret, and a gnawing hunger for more drugs which had always been his escape, a refuge from the harsh

realities of life. But now, they were devouring him, tearing at the edges of his sanity.

When he finally pulled into the driveway of his house, the headlights illuminated the manicured lawn and the imposing facade. The Lambo's engine growled one last time before he turned it off. He stumbled out of the car, legs unsteady, and leaned against the cold metal of his car. The night air was crisp, starkly contrasting with the fevered heat still coursing through his veins.

Emric entered the house, the familiar creak of the front door reverberating through the silence. The warm embrace of home enveloped him, the soft carpet underfoot, the dim glow of the hallway lights. He staggered towards the living room, where the plush sofa beckoned. Its cushions yielded beneath his weight as he collapsed, limbs heavy and uncoordinated.

His fingers fumbled in his pocket, retrieving a crumpled pack of cigarettes. The lighter sparked to life, casting an orange glow on his face. Each inhale and exhale felt like a betrayal, a dance with the devil.

The smoke curled around him, a ghostly wisp in the dim room. Emric glanced up at the clock on the wall. It was late, the hands inching towards midnight. His eyelids drooped, exhaustion pulling at him like an undertow. He wondered if Brander would ever be the man he used to be, the vibrant friend who had once laughed freely and dreamed big. Now, he was reduced to a mindless shell, lost in the labyrinth of his own thoughts.

And what about himself? Would he ever reclaim the man he had been in his youth, the one who had never touched drugs, who had thrived on adrenaline and endorphins?

'I'm cursed,' he muttered to the empty room, the words swallowed by the darkness. The sofa cradled him, and as sleep tugged at his consciousness, he wondered if redemption was still within reach. Perhaps it was time to listen to Brander's words, to fight the demons that threatened to consume him. But for now, he surrendered to the drug-induced haze, hoping that somewhere in the depths of his dreams, he would find a way back to the light.

Chapter 6
Remember me, please!

Brander stirred in his hospital bed, the sterile scent of antiseptic assaulting his senses. His eyes fluttered open, and for a disorienting moment, he couldn't recognise where he was. The room was a blur of white walls, ceiling, and the sheets surrounding him.

As he continued to look around, memories flooded back with brutal clarity: the screech of tyres, the sickening lurch as his car spun out of control, and the deafening crash that shattered his world. He remembered the fire, the searing heat, the acrid smoke, and how he had fought to free himself from the twisted wreckage. But then darkness claimed him, pulling him into oblivion.

Brander's pulse quickened as he took in his surroundings. The hospital room was eerily silent. The only sound was the soft hum of machinery. Panic clawed at his chest. Where was his wife? And Emric, his best mate, where was he?

Just as he pondered, the hospital door swung open, and a figure stumbled in. The man's hair was dishevelled, and his grey eyes were wide with worry. He wobbled over to Brander's bed, collapsing onto it, breaths ragged.

'Yo, Brander!' The man's voice cracked, desperation etched on his face. 'Man, I messed up bad. I feel like crap because I've been taking too many drugs. You need to remember everythin' and help me!'

Brander squinted at the man, his mind a foggy maze. 'I…don't…know…'

'You know me, bro!' The man's grip tightened on Brander's arm. 'You can't be such a fish brain!'

And then it clicked. Emric. His best friend, the one who had always been there through laughter, tears, and reckless adventures. Brander sat up abruptly, ignoring the dull ache in his ribs. 'Is that actually you, Emric?'

Emric's eyes widened, and he practically lunged at Brander, wrapping him in a fierce hug. 'Yeah! You do remember me. Your brain's finally working again!'

Brander rubbed his eyes, the haze lifting. 'Emric,' he whispered, 'What have you done to yourself? I barely recognised you.'

Emric's gaze dropped to the white marble floor, guilt engraved across his features. 'Brander,' he sighed, 'I've been taking too many hits. I can't stop it.'

Brander leaned back on the bed, rage glowing in his eyes, 'Where's my wife?' he asked, looking around as if she was going to appear from the shadows.

'Forget yer wife!' Emric responded, 'Do something about me!'

'I bloody care about my wife more than you!' Brander roared, 'Flippin' get lost, you dumb dog!'

Emric's eyes filled with tears, 'Brander, this ain't you,' he whispered, 'Do you even care about me anymore?'

'I hate you!' Brander shouted, 'You promised me that you would never retake this shit, and you did!'

'But we were best pals!' Emric exclaimed, 'You can't just ditch me!'

'Get out. Now!' Brander shouted.

'Fine!' Emric roared, standing up, his steps unsteady as he advanced towards the door. He stopped and looked back at Brander, 'Burn!' he laughed, 'You said to me I have too many drugs, and I'm going to end up crashing my car. Check you out, you daft idiot. You crashed your own car! I wonder who actually is on bloody drugs. BURN!'

I Tried

'Just shut up!' Brander yelled, 'Get out of here!'

'Oh, I can see you burning now!' Emric laughed, 'Don't go talking smack about others, 'cause it always comes back to bite you!'

He started to laugh hysterically as his trembling fingers grabbed the door handle, 'Next, it's gonna be you taking drugs, not me! Dumb shithead.'

Brander watched bewildered as Emric swaggered out of the room. His laughter rebounded down the hospital corridors, eventually turning into a cough.

'Daft dog,' Brander muttered, running his fingers through his messy hair.

Suddenly, the door opened once more, and a nurse stepped in. Her dark brown hair was pulled back in a neat bun, and she wore a crisp, navy-blue skirt that fell just below her knees, paired with a matching, starched blouse. The outfit was practical yet professional, with a modest collar and a few neat buttons down the front, all of it pressed to perfection.

'Hi,' she smiled, walking up to Brander's bedside, 'I see you look livelier than yesterday. Do you have an idea where you are?'

Brander slowly nodded. 'Yeah,' he responded in a low murmur. 'I need my wife,' he murmured, his eyes catching the nurse's badge that read 'Kelly.'

'Your wife?' Nurse Kelly said, 'She's not in the hospital, but we can call her if you want.'

Brander nodded, 'Yeah, call her.'

He watched Nurse Kelly exit the room, her kitten heels tapping against the waxed marble floor.

He closed his eyes, his mind drifting back to the stubborn Emric. He didn't know why he couldn't just listen to him and stop the rubbish he was taking. He sighed deeply, pulled the thin blanket over his shoulders, and settled comfortably into the bed.

I Tried

After a while, Nurse Kelly re-entered the room, followed closely by another woman. The newcomer's leather jacket clung to her form, highlighting her slender frame. Her blue eyes, filled with a profound sadness, contrasted sharply with her long, chestnut hair that cascaded down to her hips. Each step she took in her black high heels resonated through the room like the beat of a war drum. This was Brander's wife, Elara. With a swift motion, she tossed her sleek, black side bag onto the bed and made her way to his side.

'Sweetie,' Elara whispered, sitting beside him and running her fingers through his unruly hair. Her eyes were adorned with smoky eye shadow, and her rose-red lips were in a straight line.

'Elara,' Brander whispered back, his eyes locking onto hers.

Elara's eyes widened in disbelief, 'You recognise…me?' she stammered, staring at him.

Brander sat up, a smile spreading across his face, and took her hands into his. 'Yeah, I do recognise you,' he murmured.

Elara looked at him, joy dancing in her eyes. 'You're not such a mushed potato brain anymore, are you?' she chuckled, 'Dear, I'm so glad you're better.'

'Yeah,' Brander sighed, leaning back on the bed, his body still aching from the car crash.

'It looks like something is bothering your mind,' Elara whispered, 'What's up?'

Brander shook his head, 'Nothing,' he responded.

'Tell me,' Elara urged, 'Or are you just not feeling well? I do know the car crash was really bad. I just can't believe what you did to your new car.'

'Do you know what, Elara?' Brander whispered, 'Emric has been a piece of shit. I think we've severed ties with each other.'

'What?' Elara gasped, squeezing his hand, 'How can you do that to your best mate?'

I Tried

'I didn't do it,' Brander retorted sharply, running his fingers through her long hair, 'He didn't listen to me about not having drugs, and then he started to talk shit, so I told him to get lost. Straight up!'

Two days had passed, and Brander was back at his house. He was lying in his bed, the bedcover cool against his skin. Elara entered the room. 'Sweetie,' she said. 'Can you be bothered doing something?' she asked.

'What is it, darling?' Brander asked, turning to look at her.

'I need you to get some bread from the local shop,' Elara responded, settling at the end of the bed, 'Can you do it?'

'Can't be arsed!' Brander groaned, stretching lazily, 'Can't you just go yourself?'

'No, sweetie,' Elara sighed, 'Please go!'

Brander pushed himself up with a groan, 'OK, I'll quickly go.' He let out a low chuckle, and Elara rolled her eyes.

He hurried down the stairs, his footsteps resonating through the house, and quickly put on his well-worn trainers. With a quick pat on his combat pants pocket, he confirmed his wallet was secure. Stepping out into the garden, he squinted against the bright sunlight that bathed everything in a golden hue. He had plans to buy a new car, albeit a less expensive one, but for now, he would just do some grafting and walk to the shop until he found the right vehicle for his small family.

He walked down the road towards the shop, the sun searing his skin, making him long for the shop's cool interior. Entering the shop, he was immediately greeted by the refreshing coolness of the air conditioning, a soothing balm against the oppressive warmth he had just escaped, providing a brief moment of relief. However, his happiness quickly faded when he spotted a familiar figure. 'Emric,' he muttered under his breath.

I Tried

Emric's eyes were concealed behind dark shades, and his black jeans clung tightly to his legs. His golden chains swung from his neck, glinting in the light as he did a hard walk and exited the shop without even acknowledging Brander's presence.

'Junkie,' Brander muttered as he watched him pass by. But then, a thought struck his mind.

He quickly ran out of the shop after Emric. 'Emric,' he called as he saw him walking towards his Lamborghini.

Emric glanced back and slowly took his shades off. 'What do you want?' he snapped as if he were talking to a stranger.

'I want to talk to you,' Brander responded.

'Well, I don't wanna talk to ya,' Emric spat. 'If you wanna give me twenty bucks, then fair enough. Otherwise? Go.'

Brander's face fell. 'You really think I'mma give ya twenty dollars?' he said. 'I guess yer gonna stash up yer drugs with the money. I rather put that cash on ma self.'

Emric's eyes narrowed. 'You think you're better than me, Brander? Strutting around like you own the place. You're just a small fish in a big pond.'

Brander stepped closer, his voice low and steady. 'At least I'm not drowning in it, Emric. You're so deep in your mess, you can't even see straight.'

Emric laughed, a harsh sound that echoed in the quiet street. 'Keep telling yourself that. One day, you'll be begging for my help.'

'Not in this lifetime,' Brander shot back. 'I'd rather crawl on broken glass than ask you for anything.'

Emric's smile faded, replaced by a cold, hard stare. 'We'll see about that, Brander. We'll see.'

Brander watched as Emric turned away, heading back to his Lamborghini. He couldn't let Emric get away so easily. There

I Tried

was too much at stake. He quickened his pace, catching up to Emric just as he reached his car.

'Wait,' Brander said, grabbing Emric's arm. 'This isn't over.'

Emric yanked his arm free and glared at Brander. 'What do you want, Brander? You think you can just walk up to me and start something?'

Brander's eyes were steely. 'I know what you're up to, Emric. You're trying to ruin lives with the same drugs you're hooked on yourself. And I'm not going to let you destroy anyone else.'

Emric's expression darkened. 'You don't know jack. You're just trying to play hero.'

Brander's jaw tightened. 'Maybe. But at least I'm trying to do something good. Unlike you.'

Emric laughed, a cold, mirthless sound. 'Good? Ya think you're some kind of saviour? You're a thickhead.'

Before Brander could respond, a black SUV screeched to a stop beside them. The windows were tinted, and the engine idled menacingly. Emric's face twisted into a smirk.

'Looks like ma ride's here,' he said, stepping towards the SUV.

Brander's instincts screamed at him to act. He lunged forward, grabbing Emric by the collar. 'You're not going anywhere.'

Emric struggled, but Brander's grip was firm. The SUV's door swung open, and a burly man stepped out, his eyes cold and calculating.

'Let him go,' the man said, his voice low and dangerous.

Brander didn't budge. 'Not until he answers some questions.'

The man took a step closer, his hand reaching inside his jacket. 'I won't ask again.'

Brander's heart pounded in his chest. He knew he was outmatched, but he couldn't back down now. 'Emric, tell me what you're planning.'

Emric's eyes flicked towards the man, then back to Brander. 'You really wanna know? Fine. But you ain't gonna like it.'

Brander tightened his grip. 'Tell me.'

Emric leaned in, his voice a whisper. 'A shipment is scheduled to arrive in two weeks on a Wednesday night. Big money. Big risks. And you ain't gonna stop it.'

Brander's mind raced. A shipment? He had to find out more. But before he could press further, the burly man grabbed him, wrenching him away from Emric and throwing him to the ground.

'Stay out of this, you scum of earth,' the man growled. 'Or next time, you won't get up.'

Brander watched helplessly as Emric climbed into the SUV, the door slamming shut behind him. The vehicle sped off, leaving Brander lying on the pavement, his mind reeling with the implications of what he'd just learned.

He had to act fast. The clock was ticking, and if he didn't stop the shipment, countless lives could be at risk.

Brander quickly stood up, his legs trembling as he started to run back towards his house. His heart hammered against his ribcage, each pulse echoing the terror and adrenaline flooding his system. He hadn't known what his friend was up to, how bad and cunning he had become. The realisation hit him like a freight train, leaving him breathless and desperate.

The streets blurred past him as he sprinted, his mind racing with thoughts of Emric and the ominous shipment. He had to get home and warn Elara. The cool evening air did little to calm his nerves as he finally reached his house.

With a swift, forceful shove, he flung the door open, causing it to crash against the wall with a resounding bang. The noise echoed through the house as he strode into the kitchen, where the warm, inviting aroma of spices filled the air. Elara stood at the

I Tried

stove, her hands deftly stirring a simmering pot, her face illuminated by the soft glow of the overhead light.

She turned around, a warm smile on her face that quickly faded when she saw the state he was in.

'Have you brought the bread, sweetie?' she asked, her voice carrying a hint of worry.

'No,' Brander responded, shaking his head and panting loudly. He sank into a chair, his body trembling with exhaustion and fear. 'Listen,' he whispered, his voice barely audible, 'Emric was in the shop and guess what?'

Elara's eyes widened, her hands gripping the edge of the counter. 'What?' she said, panic creeping into her voice.

'He told me that a shipment is coming in two weeks,' Brander said, his words tumbling out in a rush. 'He and some people - I'm not sure exactly who they are to him - are planning to hijack it or something like that.'

Elara's face paled, her eyes darting around the room as if searching for answers. 'A shipment? What kind of shipment? Drugs? Weapons?'

'I don't know,' Brander admitted. 'But it sounded big. Dangerous. We need to do something, Elara. We can't just sit here and wait for it to happen.'

'What do you expect us to do about it?' Elara's voice was steady, her eyes unwavering. 'The police can handle that. Your friend is just a horrible man who's going to go down in life.'

Brander clenched his fists, frustration bubbling up. 'Elara, it's not that simple,' he said, his voice barely hearable. 'Emric isn't just some petty criminal. He's involved in something bigger, something very hazardous.'

Elara's expression softened, and she moved closer, her hand resting on his shoulder. 'Brander,' she said gently, 'you don't need to carry this burden. We have our own lives, our own problems.'

Brander's words spilled out in desperation. 'What if innocent people get hurt?'

Elara sighed, her thumb drawing gentle circles on his back. 'You're a good man, Brander,' she said. 'But sometimes, being good isn't enough. You can't fix everything.'

'I'm just worried,' he whispered. 'Worried that if I don't step in, no one will.'

Elara's gaze bore into his, her eyes filled with a mixture of love and concern. 'You don't worry about it,' she said firmly. 'You don't need to get involved in this mess.'

Brander's heart ached. Elara was right. They were just ordinary people caught in the crossfire of something much darker. But as he looked at her, he knew he couldn't stay idle. Time was running out, and Emric's words haunted his every thought.

Chapter 7
Check out yer jalopy!

The car's engine revved, and Brander's heart beat fast. He didn't want to crash his new vehicle even though it wasn't too expensive.

As he navigated the potholes, a menacing growl rumbled from behind. Brander's pulse quickened. He stole a glance in the rearview mirror, and there it was: a blazing orange Lamborghini, sleek and threatening. The driver, a cocky figure wearing dark shades, leaned on the horn, urging Brander to speed up.

'Provoking, huh?' Brander muttered, gripping the wheel tighter. But then he recognised the driver. Emric!

'Oh my god!' he groaned.

Emric's aerodynamic car pulled alongside Brander's rust-bitten vehicle; he lowered his window. In the passenger seat sat another man, just as bold. Their grins were a clear sign of impending mischief.

'Yo, Branny!' Emric's voice flowed through the warm evening air. 'Check out yer jalopy! Looks like it's been through a war. Burn, man, it's so crap!'

Brander clenched his jaw. 'It's reliable,' he shot back. 'Unlike that flashy death trap you're driving.'

The passenger leaned forward, cackling. 'Ugly as sin, mate! And that colour? A murky grey. Like a storm cloud about to burst.'

Heat surged up Brander's neck. He contemplated flooring the accelerator to outrun them, but Emric was relentless, matching his speed.

'Fish Brain Branny!' Emric hollered. 'Bet your thoughts swim in circles. Can't even afford a decent ride.'

I Tried

Brander's cheeks flamed. He'd never back down from a challenge, especially not from Emric. But as they raced side by side, adrenaline pumping, he wondered if this was a battle he could win or if he'd end up eating dust.

'Can you just leave me alone and live your own life?' Brander bellowed, 'I'm not your mate anymore, you bloody druggy!'

'You think you can just run away?' Emric spat, his voice an evil hiss. 'You're in something darker than you realise.'

Brander's chest tightened. He began to wish that Emric would keep the conversation going so that he could extract some information. 'What is this shipment?' he demanded, his voice hoarse. 'What are you planning?'

Emric's laughter boomed. 'You're a fool, Brander. You always have been. But fine, I'll indulge you. The shipment is a game-changer. Something that'll make me and my associates richer than kings.'

Brander's mind raced. 'Drugs? Weapons?'

Emric's eyes glittered. 'More valuable than that. Info. Secrets that can topple governments and shift the balance of power. And we're gonna become the brokers.'

The other man spoke, his voice low and dangerous. 'But you won't be part of it, Brander. You're a fool.'

Brander's pulse pounded in his temples. 'Tell me more,' he pressed. 'Who's behind it? What's at stake?'

Emric's smile was chilling. 'You'll find out soon enough. Or maybe you won't. Either way, your days of playing hero are over.'

But Brander couldn't back down. His voice grew louder. 'I won't let you destroy lives for your greed!'

Emric smirked, 'Lives? You're a naïve idiot, Brander.'

'You won't succeed,' Brander growled. 'I'll expose every secret you're hiding.'

I Tried

Emric's eyes narrowed. 'Try, Brander. But remember, one wrong move, and you'll be the first casualty.' He started to laugh, 'Let me just say two more things to you,' he said, 'Burn, man, you ain't goin' to be part of this!'

'And?' Brander asked, frowning. He hated Emric's attitude.

Emric smiled, 'Stay tuned to the news headlines to keep track of our activities at the harbour.' He started to chuckle and sped off.

A sigh escaped Brander, disbelief washing over him at the sight of his best mate. Just last week, they were best friends, but now, fate had taken a tragic turn, leaving them feeling like enemies.

He parked the car in a dimly lit car park, the flickering fluorescent lights casting eerie shadows on the cracked pavement. Brander jumped out, his breaths coming in short, frantic bursts. He needed answers, but Emric had given him nothing but cryptic warnings.

The city centre loomed ahead, a maze of alleys and secrets. Brander's hands were tucked in the pockets of his jumper, knuckles white from the tension. He walked, each step resonating in the silence. The night seemed to pause, expectant, waiting for something to shatter the silence.

He needed a distraction, something to clear his mind. Brander decided to treat himself to a burger. The takeaway was a small, dingy place, its neon sign flickering like a dying firefly.

After ordering his burger and waiting for a while, he finally sat down at a sticky table, the plastic chair creaking under his weight. He unwrapped the burger, the greasy smell filling his senses. But as he chewed, his gaze wandered. People came and went, their faces blurred by the harsh lighting.

And then he saw a teenager sitting alone at a corner table. The boy's hands kept travelling to his pockets, fingers fidgeting.

I Tried

Brander's instincts kicked in. He watched, suspicion gnawing at him. What was the kid up to?

The teenager pulled out his phone, its glow illuminating his features. Brander's eyes narrowed. Expensive phone, nervous movements. Something wasn't right. He couldn't shake the feeling that he was looking at a puzzle piece, waiting to find its place in the bigger picture.

As the boy scrolled through his phone, Brander stood up, his footsteps silent on the grimy floor. He approached the teenager, who looked up, surprise flickering in his eyes.

'Hello,' Brander greeted, his gaze fixed on the boy.

'Hi,' the boy responded, his tone full of panic.

'What's your name?' Brander asked, his voice low and casual.

The boy hesitated, then mumbled, 'August.'

Brander's heart skipped a beat. August - the same name Emric had mentioned to him a while ago. 'August,' he said, 'are you related to Emric Ladislas?'

August's eyes widened. 'He's my uncle,' he whispered.

'Do you know your uncle's plans for the shipment?' Brander inquired, leaning his arm on August's shoulder.

August's eyes darted nervously, fear evident in his expression. 'The shipment is full of secrets,' he said.

Brander's mind whirled. 'What secrets?'

August's voice dropped to a whisper. 'I can't say. But Uncle won't stop until he achieves his goals. And he'll destroy anyone who stands in his way.'

Brander leaned closer, his voice tense and urgent. 'August,' he said, 'you're not telling me everything. What's Emric after?'

August's eyes continued to dart around. 'I can't,' he whispered. 'I can't say anything.'

I Tried

Brander's frustration boiled over. 'Why protect him and not tell me?' he demanded. 'He's your uncle, but he's dangerous. People will get hurt.'

August's gaze dropped, and he traced patterns on the greasy tabletop. 'Family loyalty,' he mumbled. 'I owe him.'

'You owe him what?' Brander pressed. 'What's in that shipment? August, you're risking lives.'

August's eyes flashed with defiance, 'Do you know what?' he said, his voice suddenly rising, 'I don't know who you are. So, why shall I tell you anything?'

Brander leaned closer to the boy, his breath hot against his cheek, 'I was Emric's best mate, and we really did get along,' he whispered, his voice a mix of nostalgia and bitterness, 'But then his drugs made us part.'

'You mentioned that you two *were* best friends,' August shot back. 'So, I'm done discussing this with you because he's no longer your concern.'

Brander felt his anger boil up, a slow burn that threatened to consume him. August had a dirty attitude problem, and he definitely reminded him of a younger version of Emric. The resemblance was uncanny, and it only fuelled Brander's frustration.

'Just tell me what Emric and his posse want from the shipment!' Brander pressed, 'And then I'll leave it alone.'

August's eyes narrowed, a sneer forming on his lips. 'No, you won't,' he replied. 'I know you're plotting something.'

Brander's hazel eyes bore into his, 'You've probably got that right, lad,' he scoffed, 'And because you're not telling me and you're siding him, then I'm gonna escalate this issue further, and I'm going to speak to someone else who will give me all the info I need.'

I Tried

August's defiance wavered momentarily, but he quickly regained his composure. 'Do what you want,' he said, his voice steady. 'But you're not getting anything from me.'

Brander moved away from the boy and exited the takeaway. His mind was a whirlwind of thoughts and emotions. He wondered what Emric was up to. He couldn't tell his wife what he was planning to do because she would try to stop him, and he wouldn't let that happen. He had to find a way of getting his hands on Emric, and he knew the clock was ticking; he only had a few days left.

Chapter 8
Damn it, Detective! You gotta dig deeper!

The sun shone brightly as Brander strode into an office building, its glass facade gleaming in the midday light. He walked briskly to the counter where a woman sat, her fingers dancing rhythmically on the keyboard of an expensive computer.

'Hi,' Brander said, trying to keep his voice steady despite the adrenaline coursing through his veins.

The woman looked up, her eyes curious. 'Hi, how can I help you today, sir?' she asked, her tone professional.

'I just wanted to speak to Detective Harris,' Brander responded, leaning on the counter.

'Detective Harris?' the woman repeated, her brow furrowing. 'He's a very busy man. I guess you've already told him that you're coming?'

'Yeah,' Brander said smoothly. 'He's my friend, you see.'

'Great!' the woman said, smiling. 'He's on floor number fifteen, door number twenty-six.'

'Thanks,' Brander said, pivoting on his heel and striding towards the elevators. He pressed the button, and the glass doors opened with a soft chime. Stepping inside, he jabbed the button for the fifteenth floor. As the lift ascended, Brander peered out of the glass walls and saw the cityscape sprawling beneath him like a concrete jungle.

Finally, the elevator dinged, and the doors slid open. Brander stepped out, his footsteps reverberating in the quiet hallway. He walked over to room number twenty-six and knocked on the door. The door instantly flew open, revealing Detective Harris. His long, dark hair was meticulously gelled back in thin, precise strips, giving him a sleek yet intimidating appearance. His piercing grey eyes, sharp and unyielding, seemed to see right through Brander, their steely gaze filled with a cold, calculating intensity. Harris's skin was a tone of light brown, adding to his striking and formidable presence.

'Hi, Brander,' Harris smiled, his voice warm but his eyes sharp. 'Long time no see.'

Brander nodded, stepping into the room. Harris closed the door behind him and gestured for Brander to sit. 'Why did you want to see me?' Harris asked, settling into his chair behind a cluttered desk.

Brander sat opposite Detective Harris, leaning his elbows on the desk, his eyes roaming around the room. 'I was hoping to get some details about the harbour and a shipment that's on its way,' he said, his voice low and insistent.

Harris nodded, his expression curious. 'What would you like to know?' he asked.

'Do you remember Emric Jaasiel Ladislas, my best mate?' Brander asked, his voice tinged with a mix of nostalgia and frustration.

'Yes, I do remember,' Harris responded, his eyes narrowing. 'Why are you asking?'

'Because we had a falling out a week ago,' Brander continued, his voice trembling slightly. 'And he told me something really horrible about a shipment arriving. I need you to help me.'

Harris's eyes sharpened, his gaze assessing Brander. 'Tell me what it is,' he said, his tone serious.

'After we went our own ways, he told me something that really upset me,' Brander said, leaning closer. 'He said that he and his gang were going to the harbour. They're planning to rob a shipment that's coming on Wednesday, and I think there must be something important on it.'

I Tried

Harris's eyes widened in shock. 'Really?' he gasped. 'That's not good if it's true.'

Brander nodded, his frustration boiling over. 'Can you just check the shipments arriving on Wednesday?' he asked, his voice rising slightly.

Harris turned to his computer, his fingers flying over the keyboard. 'OK,' he finally said, his eyes scanning the screen. 'Ships are scheduled to arrive on Wednesday morning, afternoon and evening, but…' He paused, his eyes focused on the screen. 'None of them are carrying anything of importance or high value.'

Brander's frustration bubbled over, his face flushed with anger. 'Damn it, Detective! You gotta dig deeper. Emric's a bloody junkie, but he's not stupid. If he says there's something valuable on the ship, then there is.' He leaned over the desk to look at the computer's screen. 'He clearly mentioned Wednesday night, when it's dark. Are you sure you're looking at the correct shipment?'

'Yes, I am,' Harris replied. 'I'm checking Wednesday's shipment.'

'I'm telling you, you're not looking at the right day,' Brander insisted, his voice rising.

'I just mentioned that I'm looking at the right day,' Harris replied sharply, clearly losing his patience.

'I'm telling you, ya ain't,' Brander repeated, his frustration evident.

'I just bloody said I am,' Harris roared, his face turning red. 'Is your mind not stable? Am I just going to make something up?'

Brander sighed, trying to control his temper. 'But are you still going to look into this case or not?'

'No, I'm not going to,' Harris retorted. 'It appears you're fabricating this.'

I Tried

'What?' Brander's eyes widened in disbelief.

'I'm not looking into it,' Harris responded, his voice cold.

'If you're that lazy, can't you just have the FBI agents look into it? You need to understand that I'm not bloody making anything up,' Brander yelled, his voice echoing in the small office.

Harris clenched his fists, his knuckles turning white. 'I refuse to involve the FBI in your petty issue!' he said, trying to keep his voice steady. 'You sound like a child with a fantasy story stuck up his ass!'

Brander's eyes blazed with anger. 'Harris!' he roared.

'Did you just call me 'Harris'?' Harris snapped. 'You have to call me 'Detective Harris'!'

'No, you're Damn Rotten Harris,' Brander yelled. He sprang to his feet and stormed out, slamming the door behind him. His heavy footsteps echoed down the hallway as he made his way to the elevator. The lift descended slowly, each second fuelling his rage. When the doors finally opened, he stormed into the lobby, his every step pounding with fury. People turned to stare, drawn by the intensity of his anger. Even the woman at the counter glanced up, her eyes wide with curiosity and a hint of fear. Brander didn't slow down; he pushed through the lobby doors and burst outside, his anger radiating with every stride.

He walked over to his car, wrenching the door open and sinking into the seat. He looked at himself in the rear-view mirror; his face was bright red, and he felt like knuckling something or perhaps someone. The first person on his hit list was Detective Harris. He stared at the building, his fists clenched. He had to control himself not to go back inside and bang Harris out.

As he sat in his car, the city around him seemed to blur into a haze of frustration and determination. He couldn't let Emric win.

I Tried

He couldn't let Harris's dismissal deter him. There had to be another way, another lead he could follow. And he would find it, even if it meant travelling to the world's farthest corners.

Chapter 9
I can make it right! I swear!

Shadows clung to every wall, and the rain pelted down with relentless fury. Rats scurried past, their tiny feet splashing through puddles, while the moon hung low over the dark, churning sea. Brander's heart pounded in his chest as he crouched in a corner of the harbour, the rhythmic sound of waves doing little to soothe his nerves. He pulled his hoodie low over his face and wrapped his arms tightly around his waist, trembling as the cold and dampness seeped into his very bones.

Nervously, his eyes darted around as he glanced at his watch – five minutes left before the ship arrived. The ticking of the watch seemed to grow louder, amplifying his anxiety.

The thought of Emric and his gang made his stomach twist into knots. What if Emric had lied about the timing? What if it was all a diversion, and they planned to strike another day? Or worse, what if they weren't coming at all?

Suddenly, the distant sound of a ship's horn cut through the night. Brander looked up to see a large vessel entering the harbour, its bright lights slicing through the foggy gloom. He squinted, his eyes adjusting to the sudden brightness, as he slowly stood up, staring hard at the approaching ship. A thought flickered through his mind – what was he going to do to save the ship? Nobody even believed him!

He sighed deeply and leaned against a wall, mist clouding around him as he exhaled. As the ship docked, the bustling activity of people began almost instantly. Brander observed every face and movement, trying to figure out where Emric and his gang could be hiding.

I Tried

Suddenly, he spotted a man striding towards him with purpose. Brander's heart thumped against his chest. Who was this person? A mere worker or someone more dangerous? The figure approached steadily, step by step, the sound of his boots echoing softly against the ground. His thick blond fringe swayed slightly, partially obscuring one eye but not enough to hide the intensity of his gaze. The piercing blue eye that remained visible seemed to lock onto Brander with an almost magnetic pull, unblinking and unwavering. His actions were smooth and deliberate, radiating a calm assurance. As he approached, the air around him seemed to grow heavier, charged with an unspoken challenge. Each feature of his appearance, from the firm line of his jaw to the gentle tautness in his shoulders, suggested a man who was not to be underestimated.

'What da ya think yer doin' around here, mate?' he demanded in a thick accent.

Brander sighed, trying to keep his composure. 'I'm doing whatever I want around here,' he replied coolly.

'You ain't allowed to just swagger around in the harbour,' the man snapped back.

'Listen, yeah,' Brander said, his voice steady but firm, 'I'm part of the FBI. So, you better get out of here, you chav.'

'Prove it,' the man retorted, his eyes narrowing suspiciously.

Brander's hand slipped into his pocket, fumbling for the old badge he had inherited from his dad when he retired. His dad had looked just like him, so he hoped it would pass. He showed the man the badge, praying he wouldn't notice how worn it looked.

'Hey, that dude died years ago!' the man exclaimed, pointing at the picture. 'Whose badge have you been nicking?'

Before Brander could respond, a loud noise rebounded through the harbour, followed by shouts and screams. The man instantly turned around, taking in the chaotic scene as people began to run.

I Tried

Brander dashed past the man with a burst of energy, his focus locked on the ship. 'One against a whole squad,' he muttered to himself, adrenaline surging through his veins.

As he navigated the bustling harbour, he spotted a man sprinting towards the ship, something black and gleaming in his hands. Brander's pulse quickened as he gave chase. He knew he couldn't protect everyone or stop the gang's mission, but he was determined to get to Emric. The man glanced back, his straight raven-black hair falling over his forehead, framing a face that was both rugged and strikingly handsome. His dark eyes, sharp and intense, seemed to pierce through the darkness around them. The moonlight cast a silvery glow on his chiselled features, creating deep shadows that made him appear even more menacing. The night air was cool, and the distant sounds of the city were muffled, adding to the eerie atmosphere. His presence was commanding, a solitary figure standing out against the backdrop of the night.

'Listen, mate,' the man said, his voice thick with a rough accent as he stopped running, 'you better back off. This ain't got nothing to do with you.'

Brander's eyes narrowed, his voice rising with defiance. 'I'm going to make sure you lot don't get what you want,' he roared. 'You can't just hijack a ship!'

The man laughed, a harsh, mocking sound that grated on Brander's nerves. 'You'd better not get involved before I put a bullet through your damn head,' he sneered.

Brander sighed, feigning a retreat. The man watched him momentarily before turning his gaze back to the ship and striding towards it.

Seizing the opportunity, Brander slowly started following the man, ensuring he wouldn't be noticed again. He could hear the

I Tried

distant wail of police sirens but didn't want them to arrive just yet. He needed to get on that ship first.

He followed the man's path until he found himself standing in front of the massive vessel. He watched as the man disappeared into the ship's interior. Brander moved stealthily, sticking to the shadows, his heart pounding in his chest. He didn't know exactly where he was going but was determined to find Emric.

The ship's interior was enveloped in an unsettling silence, the only sound being the distant hum of machinery. Brander crept through the dimly lit corridors, every step measured and cautious. Finally, he reached the deck and heard voices. He hid behind a stack of crates and peeked out. His breath caught as he spotted Emric and the man who had taken him in the SUV.

Emric let out a deep breath, leaning against the railing and gazing at the turbulent sea, a cigarette dangling from his lips. 'Boss, I tried,' he muttered, his voice heavy with defeat. 'I just couldn't do it, but the rest of the crew are handling things.'

With eyes blazing with fury, the boss stormed over, grabbing Emric by the collar and yanking him close. 'I don't care about the others!' he bellowed, his voice reverberating across the deck. 'You were meant to oversee this operation, and you didn't come through!'

Emric's eyes widened in fear, but he maintained his composure. 'Boss, listen, it's not as simple as you think. The security was tighter than we anticipated. I did everything I could.'

The boss's grip tightened, his knuckles turning white. 'Excuses! That's all I hear from you! Do you understand the consequences of this failure for us? For me?' He shook Emric violently, causing the cigarette to fall from his lips and sizzle out in a puddle on the deck.

Emric swallowed hard, his mind racing for a way out. 'Boss, please, give me another chance. I can make it right. I swear.'

The boss's face twisted with rage. 'Another chance? You think this is a game? You've jeopardised everything we've worked for!' He shoved Emric back against the railing, his eyes cold and unforgiving.

Emric stumbled, gripping the railing to steady himself. 'Boss, I'm begging you. I can fix this. Just give me a little more time.'

The boss sneered, his voice dripping with contempt. 'Time? Time is something we don't have, thanks to you.' He stepped closer, his presence looming over Emric like a dark shadow. 'You're nothing but a liability now.'

Emric's heart pounded in his chest as he realised the gravity of his situation. 'Boss, please, I…'

'Enough!' the boss bellowed, cutting him off. 'I've had enough of your failures and your pathetic excuses.' With a swift, brutal motion, he grabbed Emric by the collar again and lifted him off his feet.

Emric's eyes widened in sheer terror as the boss dangled him precariously over the ship's railing, the cold, unforgiving ocean churning below. 'Boss, no! Please!' he cried out, his voice trembling with fear. His fingers clawed at the air, desperate for something to hold onto, while the night wind whipped around them, carrying the distant sound of crashing waves. The boss's grip was like iron, his expression a mask of ruthless determination, eyes glinting with a chilling resolve. Emric's heart pounded in his chest, each beat resonating his desperation as he dangled helplessly, his fate hanging by a thread.

The boss's expression was merciless. 'You brought this on yourself,' he growled. With a final, forceful shove, he hurled Emric over the railing.

I Tried

Emric's scream was swallowed by the sea's roar as he plunged into the dark, churning waters below. The boss stood at the railing, watching as the waves engulfed Emric's body; his expression remained one of cold indifference.

Hidden in the shadows, Brander watched the entire scene unfold, his heart pounding in his chest. He watched the boss stride away, leaving Emric's fate hanging in the balance. Without hesitation, Brander sprinted to the railing, his breaths ragged. He leaned over, scanning the dark waters below. Bubbles rose to the surface, a desperate sign of life struggling against the depths.

He couldn't let Emric die, not after everything they'd been through. But how could he save him? The ship loomed, its massive hull casting shadows on the churning sea. His thoughts raced as he searched for a solution.

Brander climbed onto the railing without hesitation, adrenaline surging through his veins. The icy wind whipped at his face as he took a deep breath and leapt into the water. The shock of the cold hit him like a physical blow, but he fought through it, kicking his legs and propelling himself downward.

The sea enveloped him, swallowing him whole. He opened his eyes, the saltwater stinging, and scanned the depths. His heart pounded as he followed the trail of bubbles, praying they led to Emric. The water was murky, and panic threatened to overwhelm him. What if he was too late?

Then, there he was, a shadowy figure, arms flailing wildly as he struggled to stay afloat. His black hair fanned out above him like a dark halo in the water. Brander swam towards Emric with all his might, his lungs burning with the effort. The cold water stung his skin, but he pushed through, reaching out desperately. His fingers finally grasped Emric's collar, holding on tightly as he tried to reach the surface.

I Tried

The icy water enveloped Brander and Emric, pulling them relentlessly into the abyss. Their struggles were futile, mere ripples against the vastness of the sea. Salt-soaked clothes clung to their shivering bodies, and the weight of despair pressed down upon them.

Brander's lungs screamed for air, his chest tightening with each passing second as he fought against the suffocating pressure. His mouth opened instinctively, but no breath came – only the heavy silence of water pressing in from all sides.

He clung to Emric, their gazes locked. The saltwater stung their eyes, blurring the world around them. Together, they fought against the pull, their bodies growing weaker with every passing moment.

Finally, they breached the surface, gasping for precious air. Brander pulled himself onto the harbour. His arms trembled as he pulled Emric onto the harbour's wooden planks. The rough wood scraped against their skin, a painful reminder of their ordeal. Brander's own strength waned, but he couldn't let go. Not now.

Emric lay beside him, face ashen, lips trembling. Brander removed his wet jumper and securely draped it over Emric's shoulders. The fabric clung to Emric's skin, offering little warmth against the chill that seeped into his bones. But it was all Brander had to give.

And then, Emric's eyelids gently closed. Panic surged through Brander. He shook Emric and whispered his name, but there was no response. Tears blurred Brander's vision as he cradled Emric's limp form. How could they have come so far only to lose each other now?

The pandemonium aboard the ship became inconsequential. Everything else faded away, leaving only the struggle to survive. The ache of loss, the bitter taste of salt, and the haunting silence

I Tried

of Emric's unconsciousness were unbearable. Brander's hand rested on Emric's chest, his heart pounding with the hope that he would stir, that he would breathe.

But without warning, darkness enveloped him. Brander's consciousness faded, leaving behind only the echo of crashing waves and the haunting memory of Emric's weakening heartbeat.

As Brander regained consciousness, it was as if he had escaped the clutches of a terrifying dream. He lay on a hard surface, his body bruised and battered. The sound of helicopter blades sliced through the air, and he squinted against the harsh light. Above him, a paramedic leaned over, saying something urgent.

'Stay with me!' the paramedic said, 'You're safe now.'

Brander's mind struggled to catch up. Safe? How had he survived? He glanced around, taking in the scene. They were on a speedboat, racing across the water. Helicopters circled overhead, their searchlights piercing the night. The boss and his gang were nowhere in sight.

Emric lay beside him, unconscious yet alive. Brander's heart swelled with relief. They had managed to survive, somehow. But questions tugged at him. Who had rescued them? How had they ended up here?

The paramedic's voice cut through his thoughts. 'What happened out there?'

Brander tried to speak, but his throat was raw. 'Ship,' he managed. 'Gang. Emric.'

The paramedic nodded in agreement. 'It's fortunate we arrived just in time.'

Brander's eyes widened as he took in the scene. The speedboat wasn't just any vessel. It was a sleek, black police boat, its hull adorned with flashing blue lights. Uniformed officers manned the controls, their expressions stern and focused. Helicopters circled overhead, casting an eerie glow on the choppy water.

Emric's eyes fluttered open, and the sterile hospital room came into focus. The pain in his chest was a constant reminder of the water that had nearly claimed him. But when he glanced across the room at Brander, whose presence should have evoked gratitude or relief, it stirred something else: a stubborn resentment.

Brander sat in the adjacent bed, his face partially obscured by bandages. Emric's gaze locked with his, creating a brief but intense moment of unspoken challenge.

'Brander,' Emric said, his voice brittle. 'Why bother to save me? I'd rather be dead than you saving me.'

Brander's expression remained blank. 'Shut up!' he shouted.

Emric winced as he shifted, the ache in his ribs intensifying. 'You risked your life. Why?'

A wry smile played on Brander's mouth. 'Maybe I'm just drawn to hopeless battles.'

Emric let out a derisive laugh. 'Hopeless battles? Is that what you think of me?'

Brander leaned forward, his eyes unyielding. 'Emric, I wanted to save you because you were my mate. My best mate.'

Emric's anger flared. 'And what do you want in return? A medal?'

Brander's voice dropped to a dangerous whisper. 'I want us to be mates again. To fight together.'

Emric's laughter was harsh. 'Fight? With you? You're ridiculous.' His rage surged. 'No, Brander. We're not mates. We're nothing. You think you're some kind of hero?' he spat out, his voice laced with disdain. 'Maybe you just want a medal.'

Brander's jaw tightened. 'I didn't do it for a prize.'

I Tried

'No,' Emric scoffed. 'You did it because you're a bleedin' fool. Risked your bloody life for what? To play the noble saviour?'

Brander frowned in disappointment as he clenched his fists. 'You're alive, aren't you?'

Emric's laughter was bitter. 'Alive, but not grateful. Do ya think this changes anything? We're still enemies, Brander. Nothing ya do will change that.'

Brander's gaze bore into him. 'We were mates once. We can be that again.'

Emric's anger flared. 'Mates? You're just a dog. You're nothing to me.'

Brander sighed deeply, the sound of water lapping against the harbour still echoing in his ears as he lay on the hospital bed. The rhythmic beeping of the heart monitor was a constant reminder of his fragile state. He couldn't believe that Emric didn't care about him, especially after he had risked his life to save him from drowning. The memory of the icy water closing in around them was still fresh in his mind, as well as the struggle to keep Emric afloat and the desperate gasps for air.

'You're just ungrateful,' he mumbled, his voice barely audible as he pulled the thin hospital blanket over his face, trying to conceal his frustration and pain.

'Oh! Is the baby gonna cry now?' Emric spat, his tone dripping with sarcasm. The harsh fluorescent lights above cast sharp shadows on his face, highlighting the disdain in his expression. His eyes narrowed, and his lips twisted into a cruel smirk, making Brander feel even smaller and more vulnerable.

'Please, Emric!' Brander cried, his voice breaking as tears welled up in his eyes. 'Can't you see how much I care about you and wish you'd feel the same?' Brander's hands trembled as he clutched the edge of the blanket, his body filled with tension.

Emric paused, his expression momentarily softening as he considered Brander's words. His eyes flickered with something unrecognisable, a fleeting hint of vulnerability. But the moment was brief. He quickly masked any hint of empathy with a cold, mocking laugh that echoed through the sterile room. 'Just shut it!' he scoffed, dismissing Brander's vulnerability with a wave of his hand. The sound of his laughter was harsh and grating, amplifying Brander's sense of isolation and rejection.

Brander's shoulders slumped, the rejection cutting deeper than any physical wound. The room seemed to close in around him, the beeping of the heart monitor a cruel reminder of his helplessness. He turned his face away, unable to bear the sight of Emric's disdain any longer. The silence that followed was oppressive, filled with the unspoken pain of a heart laid bare and brutally dismissed.

Chapter 10
My life's just messed up!

After what felt like an eternity, Brander had finally returned to the comforting embrace of his wife. Emric and his gang had been arrested and taken to prison because of the shipment they were trying to rob. However, to Brander's utter dismay, the authorities released Emric almost immediately, claiming he had no involvement in the matter. This swift release only served to heighten Brander's frustration and annoyance.

He lay in bed, Elara perched nearby. Her voice trembled as she whispered, tears glistening in her eyes. 'Why didn't you tell me you intended to stop Emric?' Her words remained suspended in the air.

Brander's expression shifted to guilt. 'I'm sorry, Elara,' he murmured. 'I won't do it again.'

Elara nodded, her sigh heavy. 'Okay,' she replied. 'I hope you keep your promise.'

'Of course, dear,' Brander mumbled apologetically, his voice a raspy whisper. His movements were sluggish, as if he carried the world's weight on his shoulders. With a languid stretch, he flung his legs over the edge of the bed. 'Anyway,' he continued, his gaze distant, 'I need to step out for a bit.' His fingers brushed against the nightstand, searching for something elusive. 'See ya, darling,' he murmured, his voice a tender whisper that barely disturbed the quiet. He pressed a gentle kiss to her cheek and then pulled away, leaving a faint trace of his presence behind.

The room seemed to close in on him as he stood, the air thick with memories and unspoken regrets. He walked towards the stairs, the marble cool and hard beneath his feet. He hesitated at the top of the staircase, taking a deep breath as he gripped the

I Tried

polished bannister. With a final glance at his bedroom, he descended the stairs, his footsteps steady and resolute.

The sun outside blazed like a relentless spotlight, casting harsh shadows on the manicured lawn. Brander slipped into his trainers, their soles worn thin from countless wanderings. The door creaked open, and he stepped into the late afternoon heat, the sun's fiery touch searing his skin.

He walked aimlessly, the pavement stretching out before him like an endless path. The city hummed around him – cars honking and people rushing.

And then he found a narrow alley, a forgotten gap between towering buildings. The air grew denser, tainted by the scent of decay and desperation. He stepped into the shadows, eyes adjusting to the dimness. Graffiti adorned the walls, cryptic messages scrawled by those who sought refuge here.

At the other end of the alley, a vivid orange Lamborghini gleamed like a forbidden fruit. Its bonnet served as an impromptu throne, and there sat Emric – an elusive and dangerous figure. Emric's hoodie was pulled low, concealing his face, but the glint in his eyes spoke of secrets and clandestine dealings. Wisps of smoke curled from his lips, the pungent aroma of weed clinging to the air.

'Yo, Brander!' Emric slouched on the Lamborghini's bonnet, hoodie pulled low over his eyes. His voice, a raspy mix of street slang and defiance, cut through the alley's haze. 'Look who's creepin' into ma turf.'

Brander clenched his jaw, the tension pulsing through his veins. 'Emric,' he shot back, 'still talkin' that shady wisdom, huh?'

Emric's grin was a wicked slash. 'Wisdom? Nah, man,' he drawled, exhaling a cloud of smoke. He flicked the joint, ashes dancing like forgotten dreams. 'You want a hit?'

I Tried

Brander's eyes darted towards the orange Lamborghini, its aerodynamic curves exuding a sense of speed and elegance. 'Nah,' he muttered. 'I got other things to do than taking hits.'

Emric's eyes narrowed. 'Other things?' His laugh was jagged. 'Like playin' house with Elara? She know 'bout your midnight escapades?'

Brander clenched his fists. 'Elara trusts me, and she knows everything I do,' he spat out. 'Unlike some.'

Emric's hood fell back, revealing sharp cheekbones and eyes that held too many secrets. 'Trust,' he scoffed. He took another drag. 'You're a fool, Brander.'

'And you?' Brander shot back. 'What's your hustle?'

Emric's grin widened. 'Freedom,' he murmured. His fingers traced the Lamborghini's bonnet possessively. 'You'll never get it.'

Brander's pulse quickened. 'Maybe not,' he admitted. 'But I got somethin' you don't.'

Emric raised an eyebrow. 'Oh? Spit it.'

'Choices,' Brander said. 'I choose a life beyond this alley.' He stepped away, the Lamborghini's allure fading. 'You can keep your freedom, Emric. It's a high I ain't chasin'.'

Emric watched him go, his laughter trailing like smoke, curling into the air. 'We'll see,' he called out, his voice dripping with mockery. 'We'll see.'

Brander glanced back, anger burning in his eyes. 'Yeah,' he yelled, his voice reverberating off the alley walls. 'We'll see.'

Emric's laughter followed him, a haunting melody that clung to the shadows. 'Mate,' he called, his tone shifting to a mocking sing-song.

Brander stopped, his fists clenched. 'What?' he snapped, turning to face Emric.

I Tried

The sound of Emric's chuckle was harsh and discordant. He hesitated, then sneered, 'Nothing actually, you moron!' he scoffed, taking another drag from his joint, the ember glowing brightly in the dim light.

Brander walked up to him, his steps heavy with frustration. He leaned on the Lamborghini, locking eyes with Emric. 'Emric,' he whispered, his voice tinged with concern, 'you don't look too good.'

Emric's eyes narrowed, his expression hardening. 'What?' he snapped, his voice defensive. 'What does that mean?'

Brander sighed, his anger melting into a mix of pity and frustration. 'Even though you don't want to be my mate and don't appreciate anything I did for you, I still want to tell you something. You need to stop your drugs!' His voice softened, filled with genuine concern. 'You're deteriorating by the day.'

Emric glared at him, taking another long drag just to show Brander he didn't care. 'Do you know what, Fish Brain Branny?' he sighed, his voice heavy with resignation.

'What?' Brander asked, ignoring the insult.

'My life's just messed up,' Emric sighed, his bravado crumbling. 'Everything I try just goes wrong.'

Brander nodded in acknowledgement, his heart aching for his old friend.

'I'm going to move to Davis Islands,' Emric continued, his voice distant. 'And I'm going to find a better life there.'

'What do you mean?' Brander asked, his curiosity piqued.

'It means 'get lost',' Emric's voice suddenly sharpened, his eyes flashing with anger.

'Fine,' Brander exhaled, stepping back reluctantly. 'If that's what you want, then let it be. You're just becoming nothing.'

Emric watched him go, his laughter turning bitter. 'We'll see,' he muttered to himself.

I Tried

As Brander disappeared into the night, Emric took another drag, the smoke filling his lungs. But deep down, he knew Brander was right. The drugs were just a temporary release from a life that felt increasingly out of control.

Chapter 11
I've lost you forever!

Two Months later

Brander sat in a hotel bedroom, the soft light of the setting sun casting a warm glow across the room. He stared out the window at the vast expanse of Florida's coast. The gentle waves lapped against the shore, a soothing rhythm. In his arms, he cradled his newborn son, the baby's tiny fingers curling around his father's thumb, his little face serene and innocent.

Elara sat close by on the deluxe bed, her eyes filled with contentment as she watched her husband and child. After the baby was born, they decided to take a holiday to Florida to enjoy the peaceful days on the beach and the happiness of their new family. The room was filled with the scent of the ocean, mingling with the faint aroma of baby powder.

'Elara,' Brander whispered, his voice barely audible over the sound of the waves. His gaze remained on the horizon, mesmerised by the sun sinking into the waves and casting a palette of orange and pink across the sky. 'I wanted to tell you something.'

Elara looked at him, her expression curious and concerned. 'What's the matter, sweetie?' she asked softly.

Brander bit his bottom lip, his mind racing. 'I saw...someone really...dreadful,' he responded, his voice trembling slightly.

Elara's brow furrowed in confusion. 'What does that mean?' she asked, her concern growing.

Brander took a deep breath, brushing a lock of hair away from his face. 'I saw that druggy,' he said, his voice carrying a hint of anger and frustration.

I Tried

'Who's 'druggy'?' Elara asked, her confusion deepening.

'Emric,' Brander abruptly responded, his eyes flashing with a mix of emotions. 'I saw the flippin' scum in the hotel.' He turned to look at Elara, his expression serious. 'Do you recall when he told me he was moving to Davis Islands?'

Elara slowly nodded, her mind replaying the memory. 'Yes, I remember,' she said softly.

Brander sighed, running his fingers through his sleeping baby's soft, downy hair. The baby stirred slightly, his tiny lips forming a perfect little scowl before settling back into a peaceful slumber. 'I think it was a bad decision coming here,' he admitted, his voice heavy with regret.

Elara let out a sigh as she reclined on the bed and propped herself up on one elbow. 'Just forget about him,' she said, her voice soothing. 'What is he going to do to you that you're worrying so much?'

Shaking his head, Brander's mind was clouded with worry. 'It's not just about his possible actions,' he said quietly. 'It's about what seeing him again signifies. It's like a ghost from my past, haunting me.'

He looked down at his son, who slept soundly in his arms, his tiny chest rising and falling with each gentle breath. The baby's delicate eyelashes fluttered slightly, and a soft coo escaped his lips, making Brander's heart swell with love. He then looked back out at the horizon. The future was uncertain, but with Elara by his side, he knew they could face anything.

One week later

Brander sat on a bench under an ancient oak tree, its gnarled branches providing a canopy of shade. He flicked through his phone, a faint smile playing on his lips. The salty sea breeze filled the air, mingling with the scent of blooming flowers and freshly cut grass. The rhythmic sound of waves crashing against the shore was a soothing backdrop to his thoughts.

His mood was light, lifted by the tranquillity of the coastal park. The sun hung low in the sky, casting a golden hue over everything it touched. Brander took a deep breath, savouring the moment. It had been a while since he felt at peace.

Out of nowhere, the soft shuffle of footsteps snapped him out of his reverie. Brander looked up to see a familiar figure approaching. Emric, with his messy hair and bloodshot eyes, sauntered towards him. His hoodie was pulled low over his face, and he reeked of drugs.

'Well, well, look who we have here,' Emric drawled, his voice slurred. He took a drag from the joint clutched between his fingers, the ember glowing brightly. 'Brander, the family man, chillin' by the sea.'

Brander's mood darkened instantly. 'Emric,' he acknowledged, his tone flat. 'What are you doing here?'

His laugh was a harsh, grating sound that filled the air. 'What am I doin' here? Man, I could ask you the same thing.'

Brander's jaw tightened. 'I'm just enjoying the day,' he replied, trying to keep his voice steady.

Emric took another drag, exhaling a cloud of smoke that drifted lazily in the breeze. 'Enjoyin' the day, huh? Must be nice, livin' the good life.' He sneered, his eyes narrowing. 'You know, some of us ain't got it so easy.'

Brander sighed, his patience wearing thin. 'What do you want, Emric?'

Emric's grin widened. 'Just catchin' up, mate. It's been, what, two months? Thought you might've forgotten about your old pal.'

Brander shook his head. 'I haven't forgotten,' he said quietly.

I Tried

Emric's expression hardened. 'All you're good at is pretendin' everything's perfect. And you act like your life is all jolly.'

Brander stood up, his fists clenched at his sides. 'You don't know anything about my life,' he snapped. 'And you have no right to judge.'

Emric laughed again, a bitter sound. 'Judge? Man, I'm just callin' it like I see it. You think you're better than me, don't ya? Just 'cause you got a wife and kid now.'

Brander took a step closer, his eyes blazing. 'This isn't about being better, Emric. All you need to do is sort yourself out. And how do you know I have a child?'

'I find ways to find out about you,' Emric responded with a smirk, 'Do ya really think I wanna be this way?' he gestured at himself, his hands quivering. 'Ya think I enjoy this?'

Brander's expression softened slightly. 'No, I don't. But you can change, Emric.'

Emric scoffed, taking another drag. 'Change? That's rich comin' from you. You don't know what it's like.'

Brander exhaled, running a hand through his hair. 'Maybe I don't. But I know this much: you can't continue down this path. It's destroying you.'

His laugh became bitter. 'Destroyin' me? Mate, I'm already done for. Nothin' left to save.'

Brander shook his head. 'That's not true. You can still turn things around if you really want to.'

Emric huffed and started to leave.

Brander watched Emric walk away, his heart heavy with a mix of frustration and pity. He turned back to the bench, hoping to find some peace again. But the tranquillity of the coastal park was shattered, replaced by the lingering tension of their encounter.

Just as Brander was about to sit down, he heard Emric's voice again, louder and more aggressive. 'Hey, Brander!' Emric called, his tone dripping with sarcasm. 'You think you're 'Mr. Perfect Family Man', huh?'

Brander turned slowly, his patience wearing thin. 'What do you want, Emric?' he asked, his voice steady but strained.

Emric sauntered back, his movements erratic. 'I want you to admit it,' he sneered. 'Admit that you're just as messed up as the rest of us. You ain't no better.'

Brander shook his head, trying to keep his composure. 'I'm not perfect, Emric. But I'm trying to make better choices.'

Emric's laughter was harsh and mocking. 'Better choices? Man, you're a joke. You think you can just walk away from your past? From me?'

Brander's fists clenched at his sides. 'I'm not walking away from anything. I'm trying to build a better future.'

Emric's eyes narrowed, his expression turning cruel. 'A better future? With that little wife of yours and your perfect baby? You think they make you better than me?'

Brander took a deep breath, trying to stay calm. 'This isn't about being better, Emric. It's about doing what's right.'

Emric scoffed, his voice dripping with disdain. 'Right? You're just a coward, hiding behind your family.'

Brander's patience snapped. 'You don't know anything about me or my family,' he said, his voice low and dangerous.

Emric's grin widened, his eyes gleaming with malice. 'Oh, I know plenty,' he said, stepping closer. 'I know you're just a scared little boy pretending to be a man. You think you can save me? Save yourself? You're pathetic.'

Brander's jaw tightened, his anger boiling over. 'I'm not trying to save you, Emric. I'm trying to help you. But you must want it.'

I Tried

Emric laughed. 'Help me? I don't need your help. I don't need anything from you.' He took another drag. 'You're just a reminder of everything I hate.'

Brander shook his head, his heart aching for his old friend. 'You don't have to be like this, Emric. You can change.'

Emric's eyes flashed with anger. 'You think I can just click my fingers and everything will be fine? You're living in a fantasy, Brander.'

Brander let out a weary breath, his shoulders slumping. 'Maybe I am. But I still believe you can turn things around.'

Emric's expression hardened. 'Well, I don't believe any of it. So why don't you get out of here and leave me alone?'

Brander looked at him, his eyes filled with sadness. 'If that's what you want,' he said quietly. 'But I'll always be here if you need me.'

Emric's laughter followed him as he turned to leave. 'Yeah, right,' he called after Brander. 'We'll see about that.'

As Brander walked away, the weight of the encounter settled heavily on his shoulders. The aroma of the sea and the rhythm of the waves no longer soothed him. Instead, they highlighted life's fragility and the decisions that shaped it.

Brander sat on a bench under a different oak tree, far from where he had encountered Emric. He hoped the change of scenery would bring him some peace, but Emric's face kept flashing before his eyes, taunting him. The more he tried to push the image away, the more it lingered, gnawing at his nerves.

He leaned back, his hands clasped behind his head, staring at the green expanse of leaves above. The rustling of the branches in the gentle breeze did little to calm him. He closed his eyes, trying to focus on the sounds of nature, birds chirping, and the waves distant crash, but Emric's mocking laughter echoed in his mind.

I Tried

After what felt like an eternity, Brander heard the distant wail of sirens. He opened his eyes and sat up, squinting towards the source of the noise. Emergency vehicles sped past, their piercing sirens disrupting the previously serene atmosphere. The urgency of their movement sent a chill down his spine.

He stood up slowly. He decided it was time to return to his hotel, which wasn't too far away. He thought it was best to take a cab to get there faster.

He hailed a cab and, within minutes, arrived at his destination. As he stepped out, his heart sank with every footstep he took towards the hotel. The scene before him was chaotic – ambulances, fire engines, and police cars filled the hotel's car park. The worst part was the sight of the hotel itself, engulfed in flames.

Brander's heart leapt into his throat. His wife, his son – where were they? Were they trapped inside that burning building? Panic surged through him, and without a second thought, he sprinted towards the hotel, his veins pumping with adrenaline.

'Elara! Elara!' he shouted, his voice hoarse with fear. He pushed through the crowd of onlookers, desperate to find his family. The heat from the flames was intense, and the acrid smell of smoke filled the air, stinging his eyes and throat.

A firefighter grabbed his arm, trying to hold him back. 'Sir, you can't go in there! It's too dangerous!'

'My wife and son are in there!' Brander yelled, struggling against the firefighter's grip. 'I have to get them out!'

The firefighter's expression softened, but his grip remained firm. 'We're doing everything we can to get everyone out safely. Please, stay back and let us do our job.'

'No, I'm not going to step back!' Brander roared, wrenching his arm free from the firefighter's grip.

I Tried

A police officer suddenly appeared, his pristine blue uniform a stark contrast to the disorder around him. He moved swiftly, grabbing Brander's arms and twisting them behind his back. 'You can't go in there,' he said firmly.

Tears blurred Brander's vision. 'Flipping, let go of me!' he cried, his voice breaking. His family was in there. Neither flames, nor fear, nor anyone could hold him back.

The inferno raged around Brander, flames licking at his resolve. The police officer's grip tightened. Shadows danced on the walls, monstrous silhouettes in a horrific theatre. Debris fell like asteroid showers.

'You're risking your life!' the officer shouted, voice strained against the cacophony of destruction. 'I won't let you throw it away!'

Brander's vision blurred – tears or smoke, he couldn't tell. Elara and their son were somewhere in that hellish chaos. He couldn't lose them – not now, not like this. Adrenaline surged, and he drove his elbow into the officer's gut. The hold broke, and the officer staggered back, momentarily stunned. Brander sprinted towards the hotel's entrance.

'Stop him!' the officer yelled, but Brander was already near the hotel. The heat hit him like a wall as he reached the entrance, nearly knocking him off his feet. The lobby was filled with thick, acrid smoke, making it hard to see or breathe. Brander covered his mouth with his sleeve, coughing as he pushed forward.

He dodged falling debris, his skin searing from the intense heat. The air thickened, suffocating him, and he coughed, tasting ash. He stumbled through the smoke-filled corridors, his eyes stinging and his lungs burning. The sound of crackling flames and falling debris filled his ears, but he pressed on, driven by sheer willpower.

I Tried

Up the stairs, each step a leap of faith. The hallway resembled a war zone – doors blown off hinges, walls scorched. He kicked open their room's door, praying Elara and their baby were still alive. Smoke billowed out, and Brander stumbled inside.

'Elara!' he shouted, his voice hoarse. 'Elara, where are you?'

The room was burning, and then a movement suddenly caught his eye – a tiny hand moving from under the bed. His heart soared. Their son! Brander crawled through the wreckage, pulling aside debris. And there, huddled together, were Elara and their baby boy. Elara clutched their baby tightly to her chest, trying to shield him from the smoke and heat.

Elara's face, streaked with soot, held relief and love. 'Brander!' she sobbed, her eyes wide with fear and relief. 'Thank God you're here!'

He rushed to her side, pulling them both into his arms. 'We have to get out of here,' he said urgently. 'Can you walk?'

Elara nodded, her face pale but determined. 'Yes, but the baby…'

'I'll carry him,' Brander said, taking the baby from her arms and cradling him against his chest. The baby stirred, letting out a soft cry, and Brander kissed the top of his tiny head, his heart swelling with love and fear. 'We need to leave.' His voice was croaky, followed by a fit of coughing. Elara nodded, her fingers gripping his arm.

'Stay close to me,' he told Elara, holding her hand tightly. Together, they made their way through the smoke-filled corridors, Brander leading the way.

The heat was unbearable, and the smoke made it hard to see or breathe. Brander's lungs burned with every breath, but he pushed on, driven by the need to get his family to safety.

As they ran through the smoke-filled corridor, Brander's senses were overwhelmed by the acrid smell of burning wood,

I Tried

the heat pressing against his skin, and the distant crackling of flames. Anxiety surged through him, but he couldn't let it distract him. His family remained in danger, and time was of the essence.

Then, through the thick, swirling smoke, Brander's gaze locked onto a shadowy figure sprawled on the floor. His heart pounded in his chest as he strained to see more clearly. The figure was half-concealed by the dense haze, but as Brander moved closer, the details became horrifyingly clear. It was Emric. His face was ashen, eyes wide and filled with terror. Each breath he took was difficult and uneven, his chest rising and falling in desperate, ragged gasps. The acrid smell of burnt fabric filled the air; Emric's clothes were scorched and singed, marks from the fire that had seared him just moments ago remained evident.

Brander swiftly handed the baby to Elara and rushed to Emric's side, falling to his knees. 'Emric!' he gasped, grabbing his friend's arm. 'Come on, let's get out of here!'

Emric's gaze met Brander's, and tears welled up. He started to cough. 'Brander,' he murmured, his voice barely audible. 'Leave me and take your family.'

'No!' Brander exclaimed, desperation fuelling his strength. 'Come with me, Emric.'

Emric shook his head, his breaths coming in shallow gasps. 'I can't,' he gasped. 'Go!'

Brander hesitated, torn between loyalty and duty. But then he heard Elara scream loudly.

The roof groaned ominously, and a section collapsed, sending sparks and debris raining down. He had to get his family out.

He looked at Emric one last time, tears blurring his vision. 'I'll remember you always,' he murmured, rising with newfound determination. He gripped Elara's hand and started to run down the stairs, the world around him a blur of smoke and chaos.

I Tried

As they neared the exit, a beam suddenly collapsed in front of them, blocking their path. Brander's heart sank, but he quickly looked around, spotting a side door that led to a stairwell.

'This way!' he shouted, pulling Elara towards the door. They stumbled through it, the cool air of the stairwell a welcome relief from the heat and smoke.

They hurried down the stairs, Brander's legs trembling with exhaustion. When they finally burst out into the open air, firefighters and paramedics rushed towards them.

'We're safe,' he whispered, holding Elara and their baby close. 'We're safe.'

As they were led to an ambulance, Brander glanced back at the burning hotel, his heart a mix of gratitude and relief. They had made it out alive, and that was all that mattered. But then, a chilling realisation struck him: Emric! He couldn't let him die in there.

His eyes darted towards the entrance, where the officer he had fought with stood, staring at him with a sinister grin. Rage surged through Brander, but he quickly turned his attention back to Elara and the baby, who were being taken into the ambulance. Determined, he braced himself and sprinted back towards the entrance they had escaped from, ignoring Elara's desperate screams for him to stop.

The lobby was a hellscape of smoke and fire, far worse than when he had first entered. His vision blurred, and he started coughing violently, clutching his stomach in pain. He surveyed the chaotic scene, his head throbbing, and sank to his knees. This was it, he thought; neither he nor Emric would make it out.

And then, adrenaline surged through him, propelling him to his feet. He hoped that Emric was still where he had left him. Brander navigated the debris-laden stairs, his heart pounding in his chest, and raced towards Emric's last known location.

I Tried

He was immensely relieved to find Emric still lying there. Brander dashed to his side. With a grunt, he raised Emric's arm and slung it over his shoulders. 'Emric, I'm back,' he whispered, his mouth filling with smoke.

Emric's eyes fluttered open, and he coughed weakly, unable to speak. Brander wasted no time, dragging Emric towards the stairs, the weight of his friend pressing heavily on his shoulders. The flames roared around them, but Brander's determination burned even brighter. They would make it out – together.

He pulled Emric down the stairs, each step a battle against the thick, acrid smoke that filled the air. The once grand hotel lobby was now an inferno, with flames licking the walls and debris scattered everywhere. The elegant chandeliers had crashed to the floor, and the opulent furniture was reduced to smouldering ruins. The heat was intense, and the roar of the fire was deafening.

Brander's eyes darted around, searching for a clear path. He spotted the stairwell where he had taken Elara and the baby down earlier. With a renewed sense of urgency, he began to drag Emric towards it. Emric's breathing became laboured, and he started to choke on the thick smoke. Panic surged through Brander as he glanced at his friend, whose face was contorted in pain and fear.

Without hesitation, Brander placed his hand over Emric's mouth, trying to stop the smoke from entering. 'You'll be fine,' he whispered, though his voice was hoarse and strained. He could feel Emric's body trembling, knowing they had to move quickly.

The stairwell was their only hope. Brander tightened his grip on Emric and began to navigate the treacherous path. The stairs were littered with debris, and the smoke made it nearly impossible to see. Each step was a struggle, but Brander's determination never wavered. He could hear the distant wail of

I Tried

sirens outside, a reminder that help was within reach, but they had to make it out by themselves.

Finally, they reached the bottom of the stairwell. Brander could see the faint outline of the exit through the haze. With a final burst of energy, he pulled Emric towards the door, the cool air a welcome relief from the suffocating heat. They stumbled out into the open, collapsing onto the pavement.

Brander looked at Emric, whose breaths were coming in ragged gasps. His eyes were shut. Seeing his friend in such a vulnerable state tore at his heart.

'Emric,' Brander said quietly, his hand gently touching his friend's chest, feeling the slight rise and fall.

Emric's eyes fluttered open, and he stared into Brander's tear-filled gaze. 'Brander,' he whispered, his voice barely audible before a fit of coughing overtook him.

'How are you feeling?' Brander asked, his voice trembling with concern.

Emric shook his head weakly. 'I don't feel good, Brander,' he whispered, his voice filled with pain.

Brander couldn't hold back his tears any longer. 'Emric! I tried everything I could to help you!' he cried out, his voice breaking with emotion.

Emric lifted his hand with great effort, placing it on Brander's shoulder. 'It's not your fault,' he whispered, his eyes filled with a mixture of gratitude and sorrow. 'But I need to tell you something.'

'What is it?' Brander asked softly, leaning in closer to hear his friend's words.

Emric coughed again, his breath coming in shallow gasps. 'I've got many debts to pay off,' he began in a low, strained voice. 'Because of my drug addiction. They even took my Lamborghini off me when I couldn't settle certain debts. And Brander, I really appreciate how much you tried to stop me from using drugs. I still remember our good old days together when we were friends. Take this,' he continued, retrieving a small diary from his jeans pocket and placing it in Brander's hand.

Brander nodded, feeling a lump form in his throat as he took the diary. 'What do you want me to do for you?' he asked, his voice choked with emotion. 'I'll do anything!'

Emric's eyes slowly started to shut, his strength fading. 'No!' Brander cried, his voice filled with desperation.

'You're my best friend, Brander,' Emric whispered, his voice barely a breath. 'Promise me you'll live your life to the fullest. Don't let my mistakes haunt you. Remember the good times we had, and make sure you find happiness. You deserve it.'

Brander's tears fell freely as he clutched Emric's hand. 'I promise,' he sobbed.

With a final, faint smile, Emric's eyes closed, and everything went silent except for Brander's heart-wrenching sobs. The weight of loss settled heavily on Brander's shoulders as he held his friend's lifeless body.

A few days after the tragic event, Brander found himself standing at the entrance of the graveyard, the weight of his grief pressing heavily on his shoulders. The sky was overcast, mirroring the sombre mood that had settled over him. He walked slowly, each step feeling like a massive effort, until he reached Emric's grave.

The headstone was simple, yet it bore the name of his dear friend, a stark reminder of the loss he had suffered. Brander sank to his knees, the cool grass beneath him a small comfort in the midst of his sorrow. He placed a trembling hand on the headstone, tracing the letters of Emric's name with his fingers.

I Tried

'Emric,' he whispered, his voice breaking. 'I miss you so much.'

Tears streamed down his face as he sat there, the memories of their friendship flooding his mind. He remembered the laughter they had shared, the adventures they had embarked on, and the countless times they had been there for each other. All that was left were the memories of those times and the heartache of knowing they could never make more.

'I tried to save you,' Brander said, his voice choked with emotion. 'I did everything I could, but it wasn't enough. I'm so sorry.'

The wind rustled the leaves of the nearby trees, a gentle reminder that life continued on, even in the face of such profound loss.

'I wish I could have done more,' Brander continued, his voice barely whispering. 'I wish I could have taken away your pain, your struggles. You didn't deserve any of it.'

As he sat there, the weight of his grief pressing down on him, Brander felt a strange sense of peace. And while the pain of losing him would never fully fade away, Brander found solace in the memories they had shared and the love that would always remain in his heart.

'You're my best friend, Emric,' he whispered, his tears falling onto the grass. 'And you always will be.'

With a heavy heart, Brander stood up, taking one last look at his friend's grave. He knew that the road ahead would be difficult, but he also knew that remembering Emric would give him the strength to carry on. As he walked away, he felt a sense of resolve, a determination to honour his friend's legacy by living a life filled with love, compassion, and courage.

Chapter 12
I promise to make you proud!

Ten months later

Brander sat on the beach, the soft sand warm beneath him as he gazed at the horizon. The sky was painted with hues of orange and pink as the sun began its descent, casting a golden glow over the tranquil sea. The gentle sound of waves lapping against the shore provided a soothing backdrop to the serene evening.

Elara rested her head on his shoulder, her hair dancing lightly in the wind. She sighed contentedly, her eyes following the playful movements of their son. 'Look at Zander,' she smiled, her voice filled with warmth and pride. 'He's growing big, isn't he?'

Brander turned his gaze to their little boy, who was a bundle of energy and joy. Zander was laughing, his giggles a sweet melody that filled the air. He was busy digging in the sand with his tiny hands, his chubby cheeks flushed with excitement. His bright blue eyes sparkled with curiosity as he discovered the wonders of the beach.

'Yeah, he's becoming a big boy,' Brander nodded, a soft smile spreading across his face. He watched as Zander found a small seashell, his eyes widening in delight. The little boy toddled over to them, holding the shell up triumphantly.

'Look, Mummy! Look, Daddy!' Zander exclaimed, his voice high-pitched and full of enthusiasm. His words were slightly garbled, but the pure joy in his expression was unmistakable.

Elara laughed, reaching out to take the seashell from him. 'That's beautiful, Zander! You're such an excellent little explorer.'

I Tried

Zander beamed, his cheeks flushing with happiness. He sat down between his parents, his tiny feet kicking up sand as he settled in. He began to babble excitedly about his discoveries, his little hands gesturing enthusiastically.

Brander wrapped an arm around Elara, pulling her closer as they watched their son. The moment was perfect, a serene snapshot of their life together. The worries and hardships of the past seemed to fade away, replaced by the simple joy of being together as a family.

'He's growing up so fast,' Brander said softly, his voice tinged with pride.

Elara nodded, her eyes never leaving Zander. 'Yes, he is. But we'll cherish every moment, won't we?'

Brander's fingers rested gently on her shoulder, his touch featherlight and comforting. His fingers pressed lightly against her skin, a wordless vow of his unyielding support. 'Absolutely. Every single moment,' he vowed, his voice a tender blend of sincerity and warmth. He leaned towards her, his lips finding her forehead. The kiss lingered as though he was imprinting his affection and unwavering commitment onto her very being.

As the sun dipped below the horizon, casting a final burst of colour across the sky, Brander felt a deep sense of contentment. They had endured so much together, and now, sitting on the beach with Elara and their beautiful son, he knew that they had everything they needed. The future was bright, and together, they would face whatever came their way.

Zander, oblivious to the profound emotions of his parents, continued to play, his laughter a sweet reminder of the innocence and joy of childhood. He picked up a handful of sand and let it slip through his fingers, watching it fall with wide-eyed wonder. Brander and Elara exchanged a loving glance, their hearts full of

I Tried

pride as they watched their little boy explore the world with pure delight.

As Brander watched Zander, a wave of memories washed over him. He remembered his joyful days with Emric, their laughter resonating through the years. They had been close, sharing adventures and dreams. The pain of losing Emric was still fresh, but Brander felt a sense of peace at that moment. He knew that Emric would have loved to see Zander growing up, and he vowed to keep his friend's memories alive by cherishing every moment of his life.

'Emric,' Brander whispered softly, his eyes glistening with tears. 'I miss you, my friend. But I promise to live a life that would make you proud.'

As Brander whispered his promise, Elara noticed the tears glistening in his eyes. She gently placed her hand on his cheek, turning his face towards her. Her eyes were filled with understanding and love.

'Brander,' she said softly, her voice a soothing balm to his aching heart. 'I know how much you miss Emric. He was a big part of your life, and it's okay to feel this way.'

Brander nodded, his emotions evident. 'I just wish he could be here to see Zander grow up. He would have loved him so much.'

Elara smiled gently, brushing a tear from Brander's cheek. 'I know he would have loved Zander, but it'll be okay.'

Brander took a deep breath, feeling a sense of calm wash over him. Elara's words were like a lifeline, pulling him out of the depths of his sorrow. He looked at Zander, who was now trying to build a sandcastle, his tiny hands patting the sand with determination.

But then, a sudden thought struck him. His hand instinctively reached into his pocket, fingers brushing against the familiar texture of the small diary Emric had entrusted to him before his

I Tried

untimely death. He always carried it with him, yet he had never once opened it. He pulled it out with a sense of urgency and carefully opened it. The pages revealed Emric's distinctive handwriting sprawled across the paper, each stroke a poignant reminder of his friend's presence.

The early pages were mundane – a record of mundane events, appointments, and fleeting moments. Brander's heart sank. Was this all there was? Just fleeting insights into Emric's personal life, as if viewed through a frosted pane.

But then he turned a page, and there it was – a fragment of vulnerability, a shard of truth. Emric chronicled their laughter, its resonance piercing the silent hush of the midnight streets, weaving their souls together. He described the taste of rain on his tongue during their rooftop conversations and the way Brander's eyes radiated kindness.

But then, as if the ink itself held secrets, the tone shifted.

Emric's handwriting grew shaky, the words trailing off into ellipses. He wrote of cravings, of battles fought in the stillness of his room, and the struggle to cut down on the drugs that had trapped him. The ink was smudged in places as if tears had fallen upon the pages.

And then, in one of the margins, a confession: 'I'm tryin', Brander. Tryin' to break free. The drugs – they're chains, but you're ma lifeline. I want to see light again, not just the fire swimming in ma veins.'

Brander's breath faltered. He traced the letters with his fingertips, feeling the weight of Emric's struggle. How many nights had they sat on that very rooftop, Emric's laughter a fragile melody against the city's din? How many times had Brander pleaded, 'Stop this, Emric'?

And now, as he turned another page, he uncovered a pressed flower – a forget-me-not, its blue petals as delicate as a whisper of hope. Beneath it, Emric had written: 'If I fall, remember this: You're ma best mate, Brander. Always.'

Tears blurred Brander's vision. The world seemed to hold its breath as if waiting for him to decipher the code of Emric's heart. The diary was more than ink and paper; it was a lifeline thrown across the abyss.

Fifteen years later

Brander looked at Zander, sitting beside him on the bed, his legs stretched before him. The room was softly lit, casting a warm glow over the cosy space. Zander, now sixteen, had grown into a tall, handsome young man. His bright blue eyes, much like his mother's, were filled with curiosity and a hint of mischief as he listened intently to his father's voice. His tousled hair fell into his eyes, and he brushed it aside with a casual flick of his hand.

'And yeah, Zander,' Brander said, his voice gentle and filled with love. 'That's the end of the story of me and my best mate Emric.'

Suddenly, the bedroom door flew open with a bang, and Elara walked in, her face pale and eyes wide with urgency. A letter was clutched tightly in her trembling hands. 'Sweetie,' she said, her voice barely above a whisper, 'Please read this letter.'

Brander took the letter from her, his fingers brushing against hers as he did. He glanced at the name on it, his heart skipping a beat. It read: *To Brander, with love from Emric Jaaziel Ladislas.*

Brander's mind raced, a whirlwind of confusion and disbelief. Emric was dead, so who could have sent this? His mind raced as he stared at Emric's familiar handwriting, a chill creeping down his spine.

Who was this?

The moral of this story:

The winding roads of life can't sever a true friend's loyalty. In this tale, despite their diverging paths, the unseen bond of their friendship held firm. Deep within, their unwavering affection endured.

Their connection was a testament to the enduring power of friendship, unyielding and steadfast.

When a friend speaks up, urging you to abandon a harmful habit, it is crucial to heed their words and set aside your ego. Such advice often stems from a place of genuine concern and deep-seated wisdom. Ignoring it could lead to dire consequences, for a true friend's guidance is like a lighthouse in a stormy sea, illuminating the safe harbour.

When shadows fall, and choices darken, the unwavering light of love and friendship glows brighter than ever, guiding us through the darkest nights.

I Tried

Coming soon...

- DID: He's Hunting Himself
- The Dance of The Shadow Boxer
- Beyond Prison Bars
- Entrapped
- Flesh and Mutations: Her Pain…His Experiment…A Dark Faith…
- Eliminated
- Horror Dudes
- Devil Brothers: Vincent Caruso
- Devil Brothers: Lysander Vale
- Devil Brothers: Dorian Orville

Explore Joseph Jethro's captivating children's books – a treat for young readers!

- Benny's Brilliant Shape Quest
- The Year-Long Adventure of Timmy, Lilly and Max
- The Adventure of Numberland
- Tito's Acorn Adventure: A Counting Quest
- Noah's Messy Mischief
- The Windy Day At The Beach
- Nina's Big Day At The Park
- Oreo And Kiki: Kitchen Disaster
- Oreo And Kiki: Living Room Disaster
- It's Boys For You: Fantastic Farts
- It's Boys For You: Great Garbage